Thad Want
Chloe's Fi
Talked Her C ... **rying Him.**

If they waited very long, he was sure she'd have second thoughts.

The idea of living without her had become an impossibility. He loved her funny little notions of propriety in public and her astonishing ability to turn into a wild woman in private—and that was as far as he'd better take *that* line of thought, if he didn't want her father to come after him with a gun.

Besides, his reasons for liking Chloe were much more than physical. He liked the way she defended him, and, even more, he had gotten used to the way she defended him, totally and without question. She enhanced his life in more ways than he could count, and there was no chance he was going to let her get away....

Dear Reader,

Silhouette Desire is proud to launch three brand-new, emotional and romantic miniseries this month! We've got twin sisters switching places, sexy men who rise above their pasts and a ranching family marrying off their Texas daughters.

Along with our spectacular new miniseries, we're bringing you Anne McAllister's latest novel in her bestselling CODE OF THE WEST series, July's MAN OF THE MONTH selection, *The Cowboy Crashes a Wedding*. Next, a shy, no-frills librarian leads a fairy-tale life when she masquerades as her twin sister in Barbara McMahon's *Cinderella Twin*, book one of her IDENTICAL TWINS! duet. In *Seducing the Proper Miss Miller* by Anne Marie Winston, the town's black sheep and the minister's daughter cause a scandal with their sudden wedding.

Sexy Western author Peggy Moreland invites readers to get to know the McCloud sisters and the irresistible men who court them—don't miss the first TEXAS BRIDES book, *The Rancher's Spittin' Image*. And a millionaire bachelor discovers his secret heir in *The Tycoon's Son* by talented author Shawna Delacorte. A gorgeous loner is keeping quiet about *His Most Scandalous Secret* in the first book in Susan Crosby's THE LONE WOLVES miniseries.

So get to know the friends and families in Silhouette Desire's hottest new miniseries—and watch for more of their love stories in months to come!

Regards,

Melissa Senate

Melissa Senate
Senior Editor
Silhouette Books

Please address questions and book requests to:
Silhouette Reader Service
U.S.: 3010 Walden Ave., P.O. Box 1325, Buffalo, NY 14269
Canadian: P.O. Box 609, Fort Erie, Ont. L2A 5X3

ANNE MARIE WINSTON

SEDUCING THE PROPER MISS MILLER

SILHOUETTE *Desire*®

Published by Silhouette Books

America's Publisher of Contemporary Romance

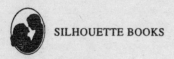

SILHOUETTE BOOKS

ISBN 0-373-76155-4

SEDUCING THE PROPER MISS MILLER

Copyright © 1998 by Anne Marie Rodgers

For Larry

If there are volunteers in Heaven,
you must be one busy guy.
Here's to trailers!

ANNE MARIE WINSTON

A native Pennsylvanian and former educator, Anne Marie is a book lover, an animal lover and always a teacher at heart. She and her husband have two daughters and a menagerie of four-footed family members. When she's not parenting, writing or reading, she devotes her time to a variety of educational efforts in her community. Readers can write to Anne Marie at P.O. Box 302, Zullinger, PA 17272.

One

WOW!

Chloe Miller froze, her gaze fixed on the window of her office in the Pennsylvania church where she was employed as administrative assistant. She'd glanced out at the April sky, hoping to see sunshine instead of showers. But the landscape was blocked by a man's body, framed in the window from hips to neck as he worked with his arms above his head on a ladder.

Her hands stilled on the keyboard, and her breath caught in a soundless "Oh-h-h," as taut pectorals stretched and flexed.

The naked male torso was lean, bronzed and packed with muscle. Droplets of sweat were caught in the curly golden *T* that bisected the chest and disappeared from sight beneath the waistband of a truly disreputable pair of jeans, a pair of jeans that embraced the heavy bulge below the zipper in a manner that left Chloe dry-mouthed and shaking her head.

So this was the carving-restoration expert the church elders had hired to repair the aging facade of the church. He looked as if somebody had carved *him*.

"That should be illegal," she muttered, tearing her gaze from the window.

The fact that she hadn't seen his face didn't matter. It wasn't often that she got the chance to fantasize about a man…in fact, she couldn't remember ever scrutinizing a male body so thoroughly before.

"You are sadly repressed," she told herself, thinking of how limited her experiences with men were compared to most other twenty-six-year-olds she knew. "Well, not just repressed," she amended. "Also too doggone busy to think about men."

Her gaze drifted back to the window and she absently appraised the torso still in full view, while her mind drifted. Did this man do carpentry work, as well? Perhaps when she got the preschool project off the ground, he could put up some sturdy shelves and cupboards that the children couldn't accidentally pull over onto themselves. There were so many safety precautions to take when considering working with young children.…

In her head Chloe could see the interior of the unused rooms in the church basement, cleaned and decorated with tiny tables and chairs, the walls hung with early learning materials and shelves full of toys for little hands to explore.

There would be a rug for story time, she thought as her gaze traced the crisp line of curls that arrowed from the woodworker's chest down into his jeans. She followed the curls back up his chest, and over a rough-hewn, stubbled jaw that was nearly all she could see of his face beneath the battered cap—

Oh, glory, he was watching her!

Chloe tore her gaze from the window and attacked the typewriter keys. She could feel a blazing heat suffusing her face. *Serves you right,* she told herself sternly, *ogling the poor man. He's probably as embarrassed as you are.*

After a minute she risked another glance toward the window.

The workman had climbed down a rung or two. An unruly mess of golden-streaked curls over which he had jammed a baseball cap hid his face from full view but he was looking straight at her, and before Chloe could react again, he raised a hand and gave her a cocky salute, white teeth flashing as he laughed aloud. The sound penetrated the glass, reaching her burning ears as she ignored the wave and applied herself to the keyboard with unnecessary vigor.

She would *not* look at him again, she promised herself.

But she couldn't prevent her mind from replaying, in vivid color, the sight of him framed in her window. She didn't know his name, at least not his first name, but she assumed he was the "Shippen" of Shippen Carving and Restoration on the contract he'd submitted.

He was rumored to be wild and undisciplined, the local bad boy. Though she couldn't recall hearing anything specific, the look on the parishioners' faces when they'd learned who had been hired to do the exterior repairs had said a lot. Miss Euphorbia Bates, who helped fold bulletins for the Sunday services, had frowned darkly when she'd heard. "A devil, that one.

I bet there wasn't a girl he ever wanted who said no to him.''

Chloe took notes once a month for the congregation's meeting of the elders. Her father, the pastor, had looked apoplectic when Mr. Shippen's name was proposed. ''He's a defiler of young women,'' he'd pronounced in ominous tones.

''God will judge each of us, so there's no need for us to judge each other,'' said Benton Hastings, the elder who was in charge of getting bids for the job. ''This young man is a skilled woodworker with a reputation for fair business dealings.''

''God works in mysterious ways,'' piped up Nelda Biller. ''Perhaps we can be an instrument of salvation.'' Nelda had a way of spouting predictable Christian platitudes, and before she could get on a roll, Benton Hastings jumped back into the pause. ''Shall we put it to a vote?''

Shippen Carving and Restoration had gotten the church job despite the dark mutterings of its pastor. What in the world, she wondered, could her father have meant?

She was shaken back to the present by the sound of the office door opening. Instantly she began to type again, fixing a pleasant smile on her face. ''Good morning, may I help…you?'' The question trailed off in the sudden silence, and Chloe's fingers stilled on the keyboard when she saw who had entered the office.

It was Shippen, the Shirtless Wonder, now decently covered with a T-shirt. He'd taken off his cap and with her first clear glance at his face, Chloe nearly jumped out of her seat in shock.

It was *him*.

Oh, this was terrible. She'd wondered about him for

three years, ever since one impetuous evening of rebellion had brought her into closer contact with him than she had liked, but she never expected to see him again. Geiserville might be a small place, but she moved in an even smaller circle within it, composed largely of her father's parish. She was hardly likely to run into a wild playboy unless she went hunting him.

Which she certainly never would do. He had no scruples and fewer morals. Exactly the type of man she would avoid at all costs.

"Hi. I'm Thad Shippen. I'm the face that goes with the body outside your window." His voice was smooth and clearly amused. He was smiling at her with warm masculine interest that she couldn't miss, but what struck her forcefully was that there wasn't a glimmer of recognition in his eyes.

He didn't remember her!

Well, this certainly wasn't the time to remind him.

She looked up at him again, feeling a hot flush spread from her neck to her hairline. She couldn't sustain the eye contact, and settled for a spot just to the left of his head. Her face felt redder than ever, but she forced the pleasant smile into place again, pretending this was just an ordinary meeting. "I'm Chloe Miller. If you need anything let me know, and I'll try to find it."

"Anything?"

She glanced at him again, startled by the innuendo, and saw that he was smiling, a knowing kind of smile that made every cell in her body stand up and take notice. He looked amused, and his eyes crinkled at the corners as his smile grew wider.

His eyes were beautiful, the kind of eyes one of her friends called bedroom eyes. Chloe always noticed people's eyes. In this case she could have been blind, and still those eyes would have made an impact. They were blue, the striking unusual sky color so rarely seen, an incredibly intense blue made even more so by the tanned skin of his face. It had been dark when she'd met him, and she'd never seen him in daylight, never been subjected to the full force of that blue gaze. The eyes held an intimate smile beneath their droopy lids that made her want to smile back, but she suppressed the urge and ignored his lazy grin.

"Was there something you needed in the office?"

He nodded, still smiling. "May I use your telephone?"

"Of course. Come around the counter." She beckoned him around to her desk and set the telephone within his reach.

Thad Shippen settled one hip comfortably on the corner of her desk and picked up the telephone. His jeans were nearly white with age, stained and ragged. The fabric stretched taut over his thighs. Through a hole along one seam she could see a wedge of tanned skin and blond curl. Hastily she averted her eyes from that leg. Her stomach was tied in enough knots to satisfy a scoutmaster.

Would he recognize her? She devoutly hoped not. The memory of the night she'd met him still embarrassed her. If *he* brought it up, she'd just die.

While he dialed and spoke to someone at the local builders' supply store down on Main Street, she studied him covertly. He didn't have movie-star-handsome features, but his straight nose and the aggressively squared jaw formed a definitely masculine face. His lower lip was full and sensual, its upper mate thin and clearly defined in a manner that curled up the corners of his mouth in repose and left him looking as if he were always just a wee bit amused at the world. When combined with a high brow that invited a woman's soothing hand and those sleepy, come-hither eyes, he was a dangerous package. She could see why it was rumored that no girl ever turned him down.

Thad put down the receiver and leisurely straightened his lean frame, smiling down at her. He was at least six feet if not a little more, she'd guess. *And all muscle,* a treacherous voice inside her reminded. Seated at her desk, Chloe felt small and unexpectedly feminine, vulnerable in a way that she couldn't quite put her finger on, but one that made the knots in her stomach loosen and flutter into big butterflies.

"Thanks for the use of your phone," he said.

"You're welcome." She felt as if the knots had migrated to her tongue.

"So I guess it's no coincidence that your last name is the same as the good Reverend Miller's."

"He's my father."

The corners of his lips curled higher. "I'm glad you're not his wife."

She felt herself coloring again. For the life of her she couldn't think of an answer to that. Before she could form a coherent thought, he began to speak again.

"Well," he said. "I guess I'd better get back on that ladder or I'll get fired." But he made no move to go.

She forced herself not to sit and gawk at him. Women probably did that all the time, and she wasn't about to let him see how he affected her. "They won't fire you. You came highly recommended."

He laughed, throwing his head back and displaying strong white teeth. "I'll just bet." Then he sobered, focusing those incredible eyes on her mouth. After a silence that lasted a beat too long, he said, "If they knew what I was thinking right now, I'd be history."

Again, she couldn't reply, couldn't form a single word. He packed more experience into that single sentence than she'd had in her entire life. Her life had been spent in a quiet world of predictable routine and studying, and since her return home, all her time and energy had been thrown into her job. Oh, she'd spent the normal amount of time as an adolescent peering into the mirror, examining her features, and she'd quickly come to the conclusion that she was never going to be a raving beauty.

Nowadays, the mirror was mostly used for making sure her flyaway brown curls weren't sticking out in all directions. She knew there wasn't anything special about her, anything that would attract a man like Thad Shippen. Could he be like this with all women?

Of course, said a little voice inside. *Remember how he treated you? With his looks, he's probably had encouragement from women all his life. Flirting—and more—must be like breathing to him.*

Still, even though she knew he didn't mean it, all the heat in her body responded to his sensual teasing. He caught her gaze with his, and for a long moment she simply stared at him.

He started to speak. "Would you—"

The door banged open.

Chloe jumped. She could have sworn Thad did the same. Reverend Miller came marching into the office, his back ramrod straight.

"Chloe, did you see where that man on the ladder got to? Oh." He paused, seeing Thad standing by her desk. "Good morning, Mr. Shippen. Is there something we can do for you?"

Thad smiled widely at her father, but even from her seat she could tell that it wasn't the warm shift of facial muscles she'd received. This one was all teeth and coolness. "Hello there, Mr. Minister, sir. Thank you, but Chloe's already taken care of everything I wanted."

She was shocked by the taunting, deliberately provocative words, but her father didn't appear to notice anything out of the ordinary.

"You're not to be in the office bothering Chloe," he said curtly. "She's busy and you should be, too, if you want to keep this job."

Thad didn't move for a long moment. Then he shrugged. "If you don't want the work done, I'll just pick up my things and let you find somebody else to do the restoration."

The minister waved a hand at the door. "Don't put words in my mouth, Mr. Shippen. Just get on with your job and leave us to ours."

To Chloe he said, "If he bothers you again, let me know."

It was a clear dismissal, but as Thad winked at her and swaggered out of the office, Chloe knew who had won. Her father didn't have the authority to fire anyone and he knew it. So why had he threatened Thad with the loss of his job?

She shook her head briskly as the minister disappeared into his office. Well, whatever it was, it had nothing to do with her, and she wasn't going to fret about it.

She attacked her work with determination, and didn't stop again until almost noon, when her father stuck his head out of his office. "Chloe, would you mind picking up some lunch for me today? I have someone in my office and I can't leave right now."

"Certainly." She smiled at him, then gathered her purse and the light spring jacket she'd worn. There was no need to ask her father what he would like; she probably knew his preferences better than he did.

As she pushed open the heavy front door of the church, she realized she would have to pass by Thad Shippen, who was still working outside though he'd moved away from her window.

The elders hadn't specified what hours he was to work, but Thad knew the office opened at eight-thirty. And that meant Chloe Miller would be sliding out of that tiny car again this morning, pushing her skirt modestly down over her shapely legs and blushing when she saw him watching.

He wouldn't miss it for the world.

She was very pretty beneath all that sedate courtesy, was Miss Church Secretary, though she didn't appear to be aware of it. She must have been a few years behind him in school, but he didn't remember her. Of course, if she hadn't hung out at parties with a beer in her hand, waiting for a ride with any guy who had an itch to scratch, he doubted their paths had crossed.

He hadn't paid much attention to the good girls.

Until Jean.

His hands stilled for a moment over the chisels he was selecting, then resumed their work. His mind, however, wasn't so easily managed. It wandered back eight years in time, back to the day Jean had come banging into his kitchen, where he used to keep his business in the early days.

"I'm pregnant, Thad," she'd announced, red hair flying in agitation. "My father's going to kill me."

Jean had indeed died, he thought sadly, but it hadn't

been at the hands of her disapproving father. Thad still visited her grave occasionally, though the headstone her family had chosen, with its depiction of a woman cradling an infant in her arms was almost more than he could take. It was still startling to see "Jean Lawman Shippen" inscribed on the stone.

So what was he doing, lusting after this prim little church secretary? he asked himself. He was poison, with a woman's life on his conscience. Not to mention an unborn baby, who had never even had a chance to draw breath.

He didn't allow himself to watch as Chloe walked into the church a few minutes later, and he was working industriously when the Reverend Miller came out a while later and drove away in his gray sedan. Around ten, he could feel his fingers getting stiff, and he decided to take a short break, maybe walk down to Main Street for a cup of coffee.

He was still climbing down the ladder when Chloe banged open the front door of the church, racing over to him in a way that seemed most unlike her. As she got close, he realized that her face was white, and the wide golden-brown eyes he thought so pretty were huge and strained.

"I smell gas," she said breathlessly. "Get away from the church and call 911." He instinctively put out a hand but she shrugged it off and turned, running back into the church before he could get out a single word.

"Damn!" Suddenly his heart was thumping a hundred miles a minute. He sprinted to the street and grabbed the first man he saw on the corner. "Get to a phone and call 911," he shouted into the fellow's startled face. "There's a gas leak in the church and there are still people inside."

As the man nodded, Thad turned and ran back to the church. Yanking open the door, he plunged into the main hallway. The odor of natural gas hit him full in the face, and his pulse racheted up another notch. Sprinting down the hallway toward the office, he nearly knocked Chloe and an elderly woman to the floor as they came out of an adjacent room. Chloe gave him a brilliant smile of relief when she saw him.

"Help me get her out of here."

"Is there anyone else inside?"

"No."

Satisfied, Thad hustled the older woman out the door. As he turned to see if Chloe was all right, he realized with a sick feeling of shock that she wasn't behind him.

Dammit, she was still in the church!

Frantic now, he ran back again. The gas smell was even stronger. He sure as hell hoped she was right, that there was nobody else in the church. Any number of tiny electrical functions could ignite gas, not to mention a match or a cigarette. He saw her immediately through the glass window in the office, grabbing computer disks and files and everything else she could find, stuffing them into a large canvas bag. He nearly pulled the door off its hinges getting in.

"Come on, we've got to get out of here!" It was a command, but she didn't even look up.

"I'll be done in a minute. You go."

"You're done *now*." He grabbed the bag from her and seized Chloe around the waist, dragging her toward the door. She struggled for a moment, then began to run with him. They cleared the office and ran down the hallway hand in hand. He kicked open the front door, and they raced through it and down the stone steps, out across the wide lawn. At the far edge of the street, policemen were pushing back the crowd of onlookers who had gathered.

Thank God, he thought, meaning it—

Behind them an immense blast shook the world. Instantaneously, what felt like a huge fist slammed into him from behind, tearing Chloe's hand from his, tossing him forward like a rag doll and rolling him across the ground. His head banged across a tree root, but he staggered to his feet, looking wildly around for Chloe.

She lay a few feet to his left, crumpled at the base of an old oak tree. Leaves and debris rained down around them, and as a stinging sensation penetrated his dazed senses, he realized that the tree was burning above them.

Dropping to Chloe's side, he shielded her body with his, feeling tiny bites across the back of his neck from the rain of fire. She had a bleeding gash at one temple, where he guessed she hit the tree, but he got a pulse in her neck. He had no choice; he had to move her.

Lifting her carefully into his arms, Thad staggered away from the tree, on toward the street and the knots of shocked people watching him approach. He could hear sirens shrieking, careering closer. Two men darted forward. One reached out and took Chloe from him, the other put a supporting shoulder beneath his arm. "C'mon, buddy, you're almost there."

But he couldn't. His knees wouldn't lock, wouldn't hold him up. As he slowly sank to the ground, his body twisted. The last thing he saw was a giant bonfire as the church was engulfed in flames.

He heard the technicians talking; before he opened his eyes he knew he was in an ambulance. One look confirmed it. He knew why, and he knew what he needed to know before he could relax. "Is Chloe okay?"

"Welcome back," said a woman in a blue medical technician's uniform. "Is Chloe the woman who was with you?"

He nodded, then was sorry as everything whirled around him.

"She's coming to the hospital with another unit," the woman said. "She wasn't conscious when we loaded you, so I can't tell you anything else."

Then they were at the hospital. To his annoyance, they carried him in on a gurney like he was severely injured, and he was poked, prodded and X-rayed about four hundred times. He was given an ice pack for his head, and some sadistic nurse cleaned and bandaged an assortment of burns and cuts he couldn't remember receiving.

He asked about Chloe at least a hundred times but nobody would tell him anything. Finally, after yet another nurse had backed out of his cubicle with a vague promise to check on Miss Miller's condition, he got off the uncomfortable bed and eased his way into the burned and bloody T-shirt they'd taken off him, then started for the door.

"Whoa, fella, where are you going?" One of his nurses, with a build and a grip like a fullback, snagged his arm.

He jerked himself free and glared at her. "I'm going to find somebody in this damned place who will tell me how Chloe Miller is doing."

The fullback scowled back. "We're checking for you. You have to be patient, Mr. Shippen."

"I've been patient," he snarled. "And now I'm done.

So just scratch me off your little list, lady, because I'm getting out of here."

"Mr. Shippen?" Another nurse came toward them, but he was in a stare-down with the fullback. Finally, with narrowed eyes and a sniff, she looked away first.

Ridiculously pleased at the small victory, he was a little happier when he turned to the second nurse. "What?"

"Miss Miller is undergoing some tests. She's been admitted to the Critical Care Unit, room 338. That's the—"

"Tests for what?"

"Routine tests for head injury. She suffered quite a blow to the head, apparently."

"When she hit the tree," he said, mostly to himself.

The nurse looked sympathetic. "It could be hours before she is allowed to have visitors other than family. Is there someone who can take you home after you're released?"

Thad didn't bother to answer her as he turned and started toward what he hoped was the exit from the Emergency Department into the rest of the hospital.

"Wait, Mr. Shippen!" The nurse's voice was a panicked squeak. "You haven't been discharged yet."

"Tough." He didn't look back.

The nurse scurried along beside him, waving a clipboard under his nose. "You'll get me in big trouble if you leave here without being discharged."

The note of genuine dismay in her voice was the only thing that penetrated his determination. He halted. "I'll give you sixty seconds to get a signature on that."

She hesitated, then apparently realized she didn't have time to argue. Her jacket flapped behind her as she raced back down the hall.

Thad rubbed his forehead, then swore under his breath when his fingers brushed over the raised lump where he'd hit the tree root. He glanced through the glass windows of the double doors leading from the emergency area, noting a sign directing visitors to the elevators. When he turned back, the nurse was coming down the hall with the doctor who had initially looked him over striding behind her.

The man frowned at him. "We're busy people around here, Mr. Shippen. I was dragged away from a seriously ill person for this."

"So sue me." Thad frowned right back. "If you'd signed me out of here when you saw me, I'd be out of your hair."

The doctor ignored him, stepping forward to shine a small light into each of Thad's eyes. "Touch your right index finger to your nose."

"Give me a break." But he complied.

The doctor lifted the clipboard and scribbled his name across the paper. "You should be admitted for additional observation, although you don't seem to be concussed. I assume that hard head protected you. If you have any episodes of blurred or double vision, any feelings of vertigo or dizziness, call your doctor or come back. Change the dressings on those burns tonight and tomorrow. After that you may remove them. See a doctor if you suspect any infection." He handed the clipboard to the nurse, who immediately dashed away again. "Any problem with that?"

Thad grinned unwillingly. "Nope. Thanks."

The doctor grinned in return. "Now get out of here and go find your girl."

Thad didn't bother to answer as he banged through the double doors and headed for the elevators.

He had just punched the button for the Critical Care Unit's floor when he heard the commotion behind him.

"That's him! Hey, Mr. Shippen!"

"Thaddeus Shippen?"

"Mr. Shippen, give us your version of what happened in the gas explosion today." A woman with sharp features and frosted hair stuck a microphone under his nose.

Another man raised his pencil in the air. "I'm from the *Valley First Edition.* Is it true that you reentered the building to rescue the church's secretary?"

"Mr. Shippen, what were you doing at the church? Are you personally involved with Miss Chloe Miller?"

Thad sagged against the wall, wishing the elevator would hurry up. He hadn't even thought about the press, but he guessed something like this was a national story just as that plane that had crashed right into a house over in Waynesboro a few years ago had been. He might as well get this over with or they'd only get more intrusive. The last thing he wanted was this crowd following him up to Chloe's floor.

He smiled at the woman reporter. "This will have to be brief."

"Certainly." She was smooth and way too polished for him as she launched into her first question. As he answered, everyone around her was nodding and scribbling in little notepads.

"When did you first realize there was a gas leak in the church?"

He took them through a short version of what had happened. From their questions, it was obvious they had talked to the elderly woman he had escorted out before he'd gone back after Chloe.

"How does it feel to be a hero, Thad?" The news-woman lightly squeezed his arm.

Thad pulled himself away as the elevator opened. "I wouldn't know. I just did what anybody else would have done. Sorry, folks, gotta go."

He turned his back on the reporters and stepped into the elevator, then pushed the button for the third floor. When the door opened, he sprinted down the hall to where signs directed him to Critical Care. He wondered where the nurses' desk was. Hospital architects must all take the same course in How to Confuse the Public. He'd never been in a hospital yet that was easy to get around.

As he turned the next corner, he came face-to-face with Reverend Miller.

Great. Mr. Holier-than-Thou.

Behind Miller was a group of people with grave-looking faces. He recognized the man who had hired him for the job at the church, as well as the woman he'd led out of the building before it blew.

"Young man!" she twittered. She leaped to her feet with amazing speed and came over to drape herself all over him. "Thank you, thank you. You saved my life!"

Thad could feel his neck getting hot. Damned if he wasn't going to blush! "Chloe saved your life," he corrected. "I just helped out a little bit."

The lady didn't miss a beat. "Well, thank you, any-way, dear boy. If it hadn't been for you, I'm sure Chloe never would have made it out of there."

The other man, Hastings, he thought his name was, extended a hand. "Yes, thank you, Mr. Shippen. Nelda here tells me Chloe was gathering up church documents when you found her." He indicated the bag the old gal was holding up. It was the bag Chloe had been stuffing full of discs and papers when he'd dragged her out of her office.

Thad almost smiled at the memory, but he was too worried about Chloe. "Yes, she was. Can someone tell me how she's doing?"

Reverend Miller stepped forward. "We haven't heard much yet. They're doing some tests and they will let us know as soon as they know anything." He cleared his throat and glanced away, then extended his hand to Thad. When their eyes met again, Thad could see the sheen of tears in the older man's eyes. "Thank you, Mr. Shippen, for saving my daughter's life. I heard that you risked your own life to go back in after her and that you carried her to safety. Chloe's mother passed away years ago. She's all I have. If she hadn't gotten out…"

"What are the tests for?" Thad couldn't take the man's obvious grief. It reminded him too much of another time in another hospital.

"Head injuries, among other things," Mr. Hastings said gently. "Would you like—"

"Mr. Shippen has been through quite an ordeal of his own," Chloe's father said. "He needs to go home and rest."

"I'll run him home," Benton Hastings said.

"Just take me back to my truck," Thad requested. "I can drive from there."

Reverend Miller gave him a sober look. "Your truck was parked in front of the church. It was destroyed." He put an arm around Thad's shoulders and turned him toward the door. "Don't worry. Our insurance will replace it for you. Thank you again for saving Chloe. Someone will call you tomorrow and update you on her condition."

Thad started to protest, but everyone was nodding. Mr. Hastings took him by the elbow, and before Thad knew it, he'd been escorted to the man's car for the short ride home to the old trailer in which he lived.

Two

He didn't sleep well. Bumps and bruises in places he hadn't even realized he had nerve endings made themselves felt throughout the night, courtesy of the blast that had thrown him to the ground. His head ached, despite the ice pack he draped over the largest lump. The spots on his back where superheated bits of debris had burned through his clothing stung and, sore as he was, he could barely reach most of them to put on the ointment from the hospital. His favorite T-shirt, washed and worn to the ultimate in comfort, had to be tossed out.

And on top of it all, he still hadn't heard how Chloe was doing. He should have made sure she was behind him when he'd first found her in the gas-filled building. Who would have thought anybody would be dumb enough to go back into that building after a bunch of files?

Well, he had work to do. He resisted the urge to snatch up the phone and call the hospital. He'd hear soon enough how she was doing. Or maybe he wouldn't. Either way, no big deal. He was only interested because she was a fellow human being. She might have tripped his switch a bit more than any woman he'd met in a long time, but it wasn't like he couldn't live without her.

Going to the card table that served as his desk in the tiny living room, he flipped through his calendar. Now that his work on the church was a moot point, he could take on a new project.

Would the church elders still want to pay him for the work he'd done? It would probably be tacky to ask for payment, he decided regretfully. The best thing to do was to get on with another job. He called the woman who was next on his list and explained that he could start her fireplace mantel restoration sooner than expected, but she wouldn't hear of him coming over.

"Take a day or two and rest, Thad. I'm sure you must be a bit shaken up after coming face-to-face with death. How about we start on Wednesday? And if you aren't feeling up to it that soon, you just let me know, and we'll postpone a bit. I feel almost guilty taking advantage of the church's misfortune, after all."

All right. Fine. He washed up his breakfast dishes and set them in the drainer, then made a beeline for the small cinder block garage he used for a workshop. If nobody wanted him to work, he'd spend the day on his own projects.

When the telephone on the wall rang just before lunchtime, he leaped for it. Maybe it was Chloe calling.

"This is Joseph Miller. May I please speak to Thaddeus Shippen?"

"Speaking." Disappointment sliced through him and he covered it with flippancy. "Hi, Rev. I guess you don't need me to work today."

"Hardly." The minister's tones sounded cooler than yesterday, when he'd been falling all over himself to thank Thad. "I'm calling to inform you of Chloe's condition, as I promised."

"So inform me." But his heart leaped into his throat. Wasn't she okay by now?

Miller went on, though he sounded like he was speaking through gritted teeth. "Chloe regained consciousness yesterday. She's doing well and is expected to leave the hospital today. There's no need for you to make a special trip just to visit."

The message couldn't have come through more clearly. Chloe didn't want to hear from him and had sent her father to let him know. She'd woken up yesterday and hadn't bothered to let him know. He guessed he couldn't blame her. Miller had probably told her about what he did to young, innocent girls, and she'd decided to heed the warning. Oh, well. She was too much of a Goody Two-shoes for him, anyway. He preferred his women ready and willing, the kind who could look out for themselves. No more virgins for him.

"Thanks," he drawled, "but you didn't have to call. I figured I'd hear about it if she up and died."

There was a moment of shocked silence from the other end. He heard Miller draw in a breath, and in a very final tone, say, "Thank you again for your courageous assistance in rescuing my daughter and Miss Biller, Mr. Shippen. They would have been a great loss to our parish and to the community, as well as a personal loss to me."

Unlike you. The unspoken message came through loud and clear.

Thad sat for a very long time with the dial tone buzzing in his ear before he slowly lowered the receiver and moved to hang up the phone.

"I'm not even allowed to dig around a little to see if anything is left?" Chloe stood, disbelieving, on the scorched grass near the twisted rubble that had been the church. Her parents had been married here when her father was just a young seminarian. She'd been baptized here and confirmed, as well. When her mother had died, the funeral service had been held at the church. Afterward, all the ladies of the parish had contributed mountains of food for the reception.

She'd always assumed that someday she would walk down the aisle on her father's arm to her waiting groom. Her eyes burned at the thought, but she fiercely shook away the tears. A church is not the building where worship occurs, she told herself. A church is all the people who worship God together.

Thanks to Thad, no part of the true church had been lost. It was a test of faith to make herself believe that, as she mourned for the loss of the building before which she stood. The structure had been reduced to an impassable, jumbled mound of brick, blackened wiring and ash. Fire following the initial explosion had quickly decimated anything that remained, including her car and Thad's truck, which had been parked directly in front of the building. Thank Heaven the church had been set well away from the street in the middle of an enormous lot. Even so, she'd been informed that only the quick actions of the fire company had prevented the fire from spreading to surrounding buildings. Yellow tape completely encircled the jumbled mess, prohibiting the public from getting too close.

"I'm sorry, honey." Her father put a comforting arm around her. "The fire chief said everything would be too smoke and water damaged to salvage. Let me take you home to rest."

"Everything...everything is gone. I still can't believe it."

Reverend Miller shuddered. "I can. I was four blocks away when it blew, and it felt like it was right next door. The vibration knocked Mrs. Murphy's knick-knacks right off the shelves. I thank God you weren't in there."

Thank Thad, you mean, she thought. Thinking of who had dragged her out dampened her spirits even more. A sob pushed its way into her throat, and she swallowed it, fiercely narrowing her eyes to prevent threatening tears from falling. She was in shock, overly emotional, that was all. It had nothing to do with Thad Shippen.

He hadn't even stuck around to see if she was all right. When she'd regained consciousness, her first question to her father had been about Thad. He'd assured her that Thad was all right, that he'd been treated for minor burns and bruises and released already. Tears threatened again, and she swallowed hard, willing them away as her father escorted her back to his car and headed home.

She had no business mooning over Thaddeus Shippen. He might have rescued her, but deep down he wasn't a gentleman, and she had firsthand experience to prove it.

Laying her head against the back of the seat, Chloe let her mind drift back to her first days home in Geiserville after her graduation from the all-girls Christian college where she'd received her teaching degree. Coming home to live hadn't been easy after having her freedom for four years. It wasn't that she'd been wild or undisciplined, but she wasn't used to having to explain where she would be every time she walked out the front door.

Then, only weeks after she'd come home, the church secretary had resigned when a brother who lived on the West Coast had a stroke. Dear Elizabeth, who had served the church faithfully for over twenty years, went to California to nurse her brother, and Chloe had agreed when her father had asked her to fill the position on a temporary basis until the elders could find a suitable replacement.

Chloe had intended to use the summer to begin preparations for the preschool she hoped to open. Instead, weeks dragged on into months, and not much was said about hiring another secretary. Each time she mentioned it to her father, he told her how capably she had filled Elizabeth's shoes and how lucky they were to have her.

One day she had been filing documents when one of the elders walked out of her father's office. "Let me be the first to welcome you officially. I'm delighted to hear you're going to be staying," the man had said.

Chloe stared at him, wondering if he was speaking to the right person.

"Er...staying where?"

"Why, here at the church." Mr. Barlow beamed. "Your father just told me that you will be glad to continue working as the secretary, and I don't mind telling you how pleased I am. I'm sure there will be no problem making it official. You have filled Elizabeth's shoes so capably we've barely noticed she's gone." The man reached for her hand and shook it enthusiastically.

"Couldn't have worked out better, could it? You have a good day now."

As the elder sailed out of the office, Chloe turned her head and stared at her father's closed door for a moment before starting across the room. She felt like screaming, like throwing something, but she forced herself to turn the knob and step into the inner office without slamming the door behind her.

"Hello, dear. I didn't hear you knock." Her father glanced up from his desk.

"That's because I didn't."

At her tone, Reverend Miller's bushy white eyebrows lifted. "What's the matter, Chloe?"

"Daddy..." She was so angry she was shaking. "No one asked me to fill the secretary's position permanently. Why did you tell Mr. Barlow I'd accepted?"

Her father pushed his chair back from his desk and spread his hands. "Why, honey, I thought you'd be pleased. It's a measure of how well you've done that the committee is eager to have you here permanently."

"I spent four years training to teach. Just because I can do this well doesn't mean I *want* to."

Her father sighed. "This is my fault, I guess. If you want to be mad at somebody, be mad at me. I've been selfish. I missed you while you were away at school. Your lonely old father's been a happy man since you came home again, and we made such a good team I just forgot you weren't wild about the idea."

Chloe struggled with the guilt his words evoked. Oh, she recognized manipulation when she heard it, but it was hard to resist, coming from her own father. Resentment rose, as well. Every time they disagreed, her father undermined her anger with his apologies and his gently worded reasoning. Even though she knew his feelings were genuine, she still disliked the way he always made her feel like *she* was the one who should apologize.

"Well, I'm *not* wild about the idea," she said, not caring if her voice was sharp. "Whether or not I've liked working with you isn't the issue. What I want to do with the rest of my life is." She turned and walked out of the inner office, closing the door behind her. Picking up her purse, she started for the main door.

Her father's door opened behind her. "Where are you going? It's past lunchtime."

"I'm taking the rest of the day off," she had said without stopping or turning around. "I need to think about what I want to do with the rest of my life."

On Tuesday afternoon, Chloe closed the drawer of the desk at which she sat. The local business and community associations had worked long hours to arrange help for the burned-out parishioners over the weekend.

By Monday, another local church had offered to change their times of worship so that Reverend Miller's congregation could use their facilities on Sundays. A temporary office had been located rent free in an empty storefront on Main Street. An assortment of donated office furniture had been used to furnish it, and she even had a computer and a copier with a fax machine on loan from an office equipment firm.

She'd spent the day doing little but checking the disks she'd saved from the explosion, purchasing necessary supplies and planning how to reestablish an office routine. It was 4:30 p.m. now, the time the office closed, and she was so exhausted she could hardly wait to lock the door and go home.

But first she had something she had to do.

In the parking lot, she climbed into the rental car she'd picked up on Saturday. Before setting her purse on the seat, though, she pulled a slip of paper from it and examined the address she had copied from the telephone book earlier in the day.

Driving out of town through the green countryside, she told herself that a phone call simply wouldn't have done the job. Thad had risked his life to save her. She certainly owed him a personal thank-you. As she crossed the creek and turned onto a narrow road that led past a hog farm, she wondered again why he hadn't come to see her, either in the hospital or since.

Then she remembered the way her father had treated him in the office just last week. Thad probably didn't want to run into that kind of attitude again. Suddenly she felt much better. She ignored the little voice inside her head that reminded her that Geiserville was a very small town, and like most towns of its size, it would have been extremely easy for Thad to find out when her father was visiting and when he left.

Past the hog farm, she entered a small wood. She was looking for a house, so she almost missed the rusting metal trailer tucked back in a clearing. As it was, she had to reverse and check the mailbox again to be sure she had the correct address.

Could this be right?

The trailer once had been an odd shade of aqua and white, but decades of neglect had faded the white and dulled the aqua unevenly where some patches had received more sun than others. Rusty stains of orange and brown oozed dry rivulets of corrosion from every seam. The pathetic structure's only saving grace was the well-maintained landscaping that surrounded it. She recognized the swollen glory of forsythia about to bloom, the variegated leaves of the mountain laurel, lilac, rhododendron and pussy willow catkins. Shoots poked from the ground, signaling the advent of iris, tulips and bushes of sweet-scented peony. Even this early in the year it was obvious that someone cared for things that grew.

Chloe checked the numbers on the mailbox one more time. Yes, this was definitely Thad's address from the telephone book.

Turning left off the road, she directed the rental car onto the rutted lane that disappeared around the other side of the trailer. A smaller building, hidden by the trees, came into view. Beside it was parked a late-model truck and she realized the pickup she'd seen Thad driving when he was working on the church probably had met the same fate her car had.

This second building was far newer than the first, built of sturdy cinder block. At first she thought it was a garage, but there was no bay for a truck.

Climbing from her car, she started to follow the driveway back to the modest front door of the trailer, but the high whining sound of some kind of machine caught her attention. She cocked her head to listen. The sound was coming from the cinder block structure, so she started in that direction.

A poured cement rectangle served as a porch. Chloe stepped onto it and peered through the dusty panes of glass, but she couldn't see anyone. Lifting a hand, she rapped sharply on the door with her knuckles.

The whining motor stopped abruptly. Footsteps clomped across the floor, and the door was yanked open.

Thad was framed in the doorway. Despite the brisk April breeze outside, he was shirtless again. When he caught sight of her standing on the doorstep, his eyebrows rose in surprise. "Well, look what the breeze blew in. What brings you out this way?"

The warm greeting she had planned died in her throat. "I...I, uh, wanted to thank you for getting me out of the church." She tried a smile.

"No big deal." He grabbed a sweatshirt from the back of a nearby chair and pulled it over his head, shoving his arms through the cut-off sleeves and pulling it as far down his broad chest as it would go. "I've already been thanked. There was no need for you to drive all the way out here."

Confusion at his attitude and a depth of hurt that she wouldn't acknowledge cut into her. But she *had* driven out here, and she was determined to have her say.

"I don't believe many people would have gone back into the church after me. You saved my life, and I'm here in person to thank you because I wanted to, not because I needed to." Her gaze dropped to the ground, and she swept the toe of one polished pump restlessly across the concrete, sweeping away minute specks of mud. "You have no idea how many people have come into my office to tell me how proud they are that I managed to save so many files and records. They all tell me that was quick thinking, but the truth is, I was an idiot, staying in that building so long."

Thad was silent, and when she finally looked up at him, a half smile flirted at one corner of his mouth. "I'd have to agree with that."

Chloe smiled back, a bubble of happiness welling up inside her. "I still can't believe I did that."

"I can't believe you did, either. I won't repeat the words I said to myself while I was running back inside after you."

She giggled. "I bet the sight of you hauling me out of there was pretty funny."

Thad smiled with her. "I was too busy to notice if anyone was laughing." Then he nodded, as if in approval. "I'm sure that quick thinking you're so determined not to take credit for saved the church a tremendous amount of trouble. Just think what it would have been like to have to try to piece together all those records."

She shuddered in mock dread. "That was all I could think of. I learned early to be practical. It isn't a habit that goes away."

He straightened away from the door frame and stepped outside with her. The stoop immediately seemed too small and crowded, though she moved to one side to give him space. Thad took a deep breath of the moist spring air and loudly exhaled it. "Ah, this is great. I needed a break." Then he turned to pin her with a penetrating gaze again. "Why did you learn to be practical early? And what's 'early' mean?"

Chloe shook her head, fondly recalling her childhood. "My father spent most of his life with his head in the clouds. Somebody had to be practical."

"How about your mother? Didn't she fill the bill?"

"My mother died when I was nine. Daddy wasn't cut out for running a household, especially one with a child. He had a hard time remembering essential details like grocery shopping and paying bills. I think he simply had too many other thoughts in his head."

"Being a pastor doesn't leave room for parenting?" Thad appeared to be genuinely curious rather than critical.

"Daddy takes good care of those who need him in our congregation, even when they don't realize they need him. I was part of his team, rather than one of his responsibilities, and I liked it that way."

Thad had sobered at her last words. Now he looked away from her, squinting at the bright light dappling the woods beyond his garden. "Part of his team...that sounds cozy. My childhood was more of a solo flight."

How did one respond to that? Chloe paused, searching for the right thing to say. But there was no right thing. The gossip she'd heard about him sprang into her head, that he'd run wild as a child, that his mother had entertained men on a regular basis, which was the church folks' way of saying she slept around. Chloe stood in tongue-tied silence, and after a moment he glanced back at her, his expression mocking.

"Sorry if my upbringing offends your Christian sensibilities. Unfortunately, everybody doesn't live by your high standards."

"I'm not offended." She felt color springing to her cheeks. "I was merely weighing my words. You have this prickly attitude that makes me afraid *I'll* offend *you.* I was thinking that flying solo is a really tough way to grow up."

"It is." Thad exhaled, absently running a hand over his chest, but he didn't volunteer anything more. "Sorry. I guess I'm a little defensive."

A little? She almost laughed aloud. Thad waved his indifference to people's opinion in their faces like a matador challenging a bull. But since he'd just apologized, she supposed it wasn't the time to tell him so.

"So what are you working on now that you don't have to remodel the church?" Perhaps a change of subject was for the best.

He glanced behind him into his wood shop. "I have several other things lined up to start on, but today I was

just hacking around with some different techniques.''
He grimaced. ''I don't imagine the church will want me
to finish that job now.'' He chuckled, inviting her to
laugh with him.

It was good to see him lighthearted. She chuckled,
too, but after a moment the laughter died away and she
was left replaying those frantic, fearful moments when
she'd thought they weren't going to make it out of the
church in time. Thad was holding her gaze with his. His
face sobered, and she knew he was sharing the memo-
ries.

''Thank you,'' she whispered as her lower lip began
to tremble. If he hadn't come after her, she wouldn't be
here now, feeling the heat from his body—

''Don't think about it.'' Thad raised one hand and
covered her mouth with his palm, pressing firmly for a
moment. ''We made it. That's all that counts.'' Then
he dropped his hand, reaching for her palm and lacing
his fingers through hers.

She stared at their joined hands. His curled around
her fingers, almost hiding them. His skin was hot and
dry, the palm tough from the work he did. The very
center was wet where it had pressed against her lips,
and a strange sensation tickled the pit of her stomach
as a mental image of those lips sliding onto hers slipped
into her head.

''So. Did you drive out here just to thank me, or do
you have something else to do in the area?'' Thad was
speaking to her but he wasn't looking at her eyes. Instead, his gaze was fixed on her lips. Sensation magnified. She was conscious of her breath rushing in and
out over those lips, of a quivering excitement in the
muscles of her stomach. Belatedly she remembered that

she had come only to thank him, that her father would be expecting her for dinner any moment.

"I have to leave." Her voice sounded strange to her, low and strangled, but he must not have noticed. He stepped off the stoop, her hand still firmly gripped in his, and led her toward her car.

In her mind she could still feel the rough, warm press of his palm across her lips. She'd wanted desperately to lick them, to taste him so she could carry the taste with her when she left. But a combination of shyness and common sense had held her back, and she knew she would have been asking for trouble.

And of course, the last thing she wanted was trouble. Thad Shippen was trouble with a capital *T* and if she had any sense she'd get out of here right now. She'd done her duty and proffered her thanks. Her obligation was ended.

Too bad her fascination wasn't.

When Thad stopped beside the driver's door of her car she looked around, surprised. She wasn't entirely sure how she'd gotten here, but she had the awful suspicion that she might have floated. All she could think about was the way his hand cradled her much smaller one; the rough, callused warmth of his fingers where they were linked with hers; the way that hand and its mate would feel exploring her smooth, sensitive skin.

She couldn't look at Thad, afraid he might read her thoughts. Then her flustered senses jangled a warning, and she did glance up at him. He was smiling down at her as he lifted her hand to his lips. His lips. She was riveted by the sight of those chiseled male lips forming a kiss. Then he lightly pressed his mouth to the very tip of her middle finger. She wanted to jerk away—no, she wanted him to keep touching her like that. Never in her life had she been around a man who drew her as this man did. As she stared at him, she felt her heartbeat speed up. The tip of his tongue whisked across her fingertip, moistening the pad, and her breath caught in her throat, then rushed out on a sigh. Her knees felt weak. At the apex of her thighs, a warm throbbing awoke. She longed to press her body against his and...*and what, Chloe?*

Thad raised his other hand and gently lifted her chin with his index finger. She raised her eyes to his and found in them an answer to her longing.

"Would you like to stay for a while?" His voice was a low growl that made her toes curl inside her shoes.

She knew what he meant, and she knew that she shouldn't be giving this man the impression that she was the kind of girl who would—would stay. She shook her head. "I can't."

Thad smiled as if he'd expected her answer. "Then you'd better get out of here while you still have a choice, sweet thing." He dropped his hands away from her and stepped back, hooking his thumbs in the back pockets of his jeans.

Chloe stood dumbly for a minute, then mentally shook herself and reached for the handle of her car door. She wasn't interested in a fling with Thad Shippen. There was a big difference between thinking someone was attractive and deciding to engage in premarital se— *oh, my goodness!* Chloe's eyes widened. Her gaze had wandered down his body involuntarily until it reached the faded blue jeans that fit him like a second skin. The bulge distending the zipper shocked her silly, leaving no doubt in her mind what he was thinking. Her gaze flew back to his face and she could see the smirk beginning.

"Like what you see?" Thad was openly laughing now.

Hastily she yanked open the door and slid into her car, slipping it into gear and reversing out of his driveway. As she drove away, she tried to work up outrage, anger, disgust...but all she could think was that if he had taken her inside that trailer she'd be learning right now what would assuage this anxious yearning within her.

Three

Three

Every time he came through town the following week, she was in his way. He couldn't avoid her if he tried.

At least, that's what he told himself as he drove at a snail's pace past the storefront on Main Street where the church had set up a temporary office in the donated space. He tapped his brake, slowing a little more. She'd been seated at her desk all morning, intent on some sheaf of papers. Sure would be nice if she'd get up and sashay over to the filing cabinet so he could watch her.

The guy behind him honked his horn impatiently, and at the sound of the horn blaring, Chloe glanced up from what she was doing at the desk that looked out toward the street.

Quickly he slouched down in the rental truck, turning his face away. He hoped she hadn't seen him. She was liable to think he was watching her or something. It wasn't his fault that he'd had to make four trips to the hardware store this morning. And it sure wasn't his fault that the hardware store was two doors down from where she was working.

No, he didn't want her to get the wrong impression. He found her attractive, but she wasn't his type. No, his type wasn't afraid to show off feminine charms. He liked women with bold eyes and tight clothes, women who knew the score and the rules of the game. Jean had been the only exception to that, and she'd fooled him when he'd first met her...a nice girl posing as a party babe.

Still, he'd been interested when he first laid eyes on Chloe through that window at the old church. *Very* interested. She'd been watching him, and when she'd seen him looking back, she'd become all flustered and turned five shades of pretty pink.

Pretty. It was a good word for her. Chloe was pretty in an old-fashioned, quietly elegant, peaches-and-cream way that was rarely seen anymore, a ladylike prettiness that was distinctly less than fashionable in today's world of carefully rumpled, clumpy-shoes-and-shapeless-clothes glamour. If there was one thing Thad knew about, it was women. Courtesy of his mother, he'd been raised around women who spent big bucks and long hours trying to achieve beauty.

He could spot mascara at fifty yards and knew exactly how much time and mousse it took to create a headful of tousled curls that invited a man to dream about what they'd look like spilled across a pillow while he ravished their owner. He knew what a petite size in women's clothing was and if a perfume was musk or floral based, whether nail polish was frosted or crème and when a woman was wearing a push-up bra to help enhance what Mother Nature had skimped on.

Mother Nature hadn't skimped on Chloe, he remembered. Beneath those modestly buttoned blouses she wore with her prim suits was the figure of a goddess. The day she'd come to see him, she'd left her suit jacket in the car. He'd been so distracted by the firm mounds beneath the ivory silk of her short-sleeved blouse, he'd barely heard half of what she'd said.

For a few insane moments, he'd actually contemplated asking her out. But a few minutes into that fantasy, he'd come to his senses. Chloe was a sweet, sheltered, minister's daughter. And not just any minister, either, but the one who had conducted his wife's funeral service. She also was modest and courteous and kind to everybody—kind enough to make a big deal out of him saving her life, when she had to know her father would have thanked him already.

He, on the other hand, had never been sweet or sheltered, and he seriously doubted any woman anywhere would consider him modest, courteous or kind. A sudden vision of Chloe's face when he'd kissed her palm sailed into his head and with no more encouragement than that, his body began to respond as strongly as it had when she'd been standing right in front of him, confusion and arousal clouding her wide eyes. He'd wanted to pull up her modest skirts right there and bare every long, silky inch of her to his seeking hands—and the knowledge that he couldn't had frustrated him in a way he hadn't experienced in years. It had been rude and cruel to tease her like he had, but he'd wanted to shock her into leaving before he gave in to the inner voice shouting at him to haul her out of her car and into the trailer.

He could still see the way her pupils had dilated in shock as she'd realized she was looking at a fully aroused man. And she had been shocked, no question about it. It was just one more difference between them. Most of the women he knew would have laughed and snuggled right up.

Hell, he'd been raised watching his mother do exactly that. Chloe was the antithesis of his mother, genteel rather than coarse. He sensed that beneath her sedate surface there might be a smouldering ember waiting to burst into flame, but unlike his mother, she wouldn't allow the nearest man to feed her fire. No, Little Miss Miller would undoubtedly wait for Mr. Deadly Dull But Approved by Daddy and get a ring on her finger before she let anyone close enough to get warm. She and his mother couldn't be less alike.

But as he circled around through the high school parking lot and turned the rental truck back down Main Street one more time, he had to admit that in one way, Chloe and his mother did share something in common. Chloe was kind to everyone. That had been one of the first things he'd noticed about her. Just like his mother. She might have been easy with her favors before she'd gotten old and ill, but she'd always had a big heart.

She'd do anything for a friend who needed her, anything for him. He might have had a mother who liked the male of the species a mite too much, but he'd been loved.

As he drove past the temporary church office yet again, a car swung out of a parking space just ahead of him.

Fate.

He'd always been one to step right up when Lady Luck called. That empty parking space was a clear directive. He was supposed to stop and talk to Chloe. In fact, maybe he was even supposed to ask her out.

He considered the idea for a moment, pretending it was the first time it had occurred to him. Maybe she wasn't normally his type nor he hers, but what the heck.

Why else would that parking spot have opened up at that exact moment in time?

He sensed the exact moment she saw him. He didn't know why, but as he stepped out of the truck and popped a quarter into the meter, he knew she was watching him. He felt her...awareness of him as clearly as if she'd made eye contact.

Which she hadn't. No, she kept her head bent over her desk until the moment he stepped through the door. Then she looked up, a smile on her face. He didn't particularly like the smile. It was friendly, but professional, and too impersonal for the way he felt. He wanted her to smile at him like she meant it. Like he was someone important enough to merit an intimate exchange of expressions.

"Hi." He probably should say something else, but he couldn't quite think of what.

"Hello." Her smile did warm, then, as he stood like a dolt in the middle of her office with a big silly grin plastered all over his face.

"I...uh, was just coming through and thought I'd stop for a minute." Where was his poise, his finesse? He was pretty smooth most of the time but today, *smooth* seemed to have been replaced by *distinctly rough and bumpy.*

"I'm glad you did." Her smile warmed even more, but then she glanced over his shoulder as the door opened again, and the expression on her face faded to what he could swear was dismay, which she quickly changed as she said, "Hello, Daddy. I'm sure you remember Mr. Shippen."

Reverend Miller made a production out of hanging his raincoat up, before turning and offering a hand to Thad. "Thaddeus."

Thad extended his own, resisting the urge to squeeze the older man's hand in a handshake that would break a few bones. "Hello, Reverend Miller."

"No decisions have been made yet about when or whether the church will be restored," the pastor informed him. "Someone from the building committee will be in touch with you if your services are needed. In the meantime, Mr. Hastings can answer any questions you have." Reverend Miller stood stolidly in front of Chloe, as if she were a nineteenth-century virgin and Thad were a rake of the worst repute.

Which, come to think of it, probably wasn't all that far from the truth.

Thad merely smiled as Chloe's father attempted to outstare him. "I'm not here on business."

The minister's white eyebrows lifted. "Oh? Are you in need of spiritual assistance?"

The mere thought of that was too much to take. Thad allowed a chuckle to escape before he noticed Reverend Miller's expression, and the look sobered him suddenly. "Anyone with a dying parent is in need of spiritual assistance, Rev, but I'll take a raincheck on your offer, if that's what it was."

An awkward silence fell. Chloe and her father wore nearly identical expressions of shock that rapidly turned to sympathy. The pastor said, "Please accept my sympathies, Thaddeus. I was unaware that there was illness in your family."

Chloe's eyes were huge and compassionate. She stepped around her father and laid a hand on Thad's arm. "Is it your mother or father?"

He could have shocked her again then, but he didn't tell her he had no idea who his father was. He merely said, "My mother."

Chloe wasn't satisfied, though. "What's wrong with your mother?"

"She has cancer." Might as well be blunt, he decided. "She's been fighting it for several years, but she's about run out of options and energy. All I can do now is keep her comfortable as much as possible."

Chloe's face softened in sympathy. "I'm sorry. That's a difficult thing for a family to suffer through." Then her expression turned thoughtful. "Does she have a church affiliation?"

Thad stifled the urge to laugh again. She must not know about his mother, or she'd hardly have asked *that*. He shook his head and smiled gently at her, touched by the question in a way he hadn't expected. "No."

"Well, then!" Chloe turned to her father with a radiant smile. "Daddy, you have an opening in your visitation schedule today. You could visit Mrs. Shippen."

The minister hesitated.

Thad couldn't resist. "It's *Miss* Shippen, not Mrs."

Chloe never blinked. "Then you can visit Miss Shippen around three o'clock. Do you think that would suit?" She looked at Thad with a question in her eyes, and he realized abruptly that she was serious, that she really expected her father to visit his mother.

He couldn't do this any longer, as much as he enjoyed needling the prudish, judgmental old man. "I don't think that's a good idea," he said to Chloe. Then he looked at her father. "It's all right. No one expects you to minister to an old hooker."

Chloe gasped. "Thad! What a disrespectful way to

refer to your own mother. Of course my father will be glad to visit her."

Reverend Miller nodded. Raising his gaze to Thad's, he said, "Thaddeus, if your mother wouldn't object to a ministerial visit, I'd be happy to see her this afternoon. We also will add her name to our prayer chain." Sincerity sounded in his tone, and his steady gaze looked almost remorseful.

Thad felt like somebody had hit him over the head. Since when had a *minister* wanted to have anything to do with his family? "I guess she'd enjoy that, sir...I think she'd like it very much."

"Good. Tell her I'll be there at three, then." Recovering his aplomb, the reverend smiled at Thad, clearly waiting for him to take his leave.

Thad smiled back. He'd come in here to ask Chloe out, and he wasn't leaving without doing just that. Regardless of her father. After all, it wasn't like he was marrying her. What a thought—having that guy for a father-in-law.

Keeping the bland smile firmly in place, he waited.

Chloe turned away from the two men and plucked something from her desk. "Here are your messages, Daddy. The director of the youth conference wants you to call her this afternoon if you have time."

Her father took the sheaf of pink papers from Chloe without looking away from Thad. Finally he turned to Chloe. "Thank you. Don't forget, those bulletins have to be finished today."

"They're already done." She smiled sweetly as her father at last turned and stumped past her into the office at the back.

When the door closed behind him, she smiled at Thad

again. "I must apologize for Daddy. He's usually not so...abrupt. This change has him all upset."

He wanted to point out that her father had been rude to him since their first meeting, but he decided that might not be the best approach. "It looks like you have a pretty good handle on things here," he said instead.

"People have been wonderful." She indicated the furnished room with a sweep of her hand. "We've had everything I could possibly need donated." She cocked her head and looked at him questioningly. "What did you stop by for?"

He thought about lying, about working around to his point gradually, but he figured his time was limited. The rev might come storming out of his office any minute now.

"I want you to have dinner with me," he said baldly.

Chloe's eyes widened and she blinked. "I beg your pardon?"

Maybe he should have asked, instead of giving her an edict. "I'm asking you out," he said again. "Would you like to have dinner with me?"

She hesitated.

His heart sank.

"Well," she began, "I don't—"

"Just forget it." Sudden hurt blossomed in his chest. Unable to allow it to surface, he channeled it into anger, cutting off the refusal he could see forming on her face. "I've spent my life being ignored by half this town. I thought maybe you were different. I was wrong." He pivoted and was halfway out the door before she could marshall a word in her own defense. "Tell your old man not to bother visiting my old lady. She doesn't need to feel any worse than she already does."

* * *

It was a good thing she'd finished the most urgent work on the bulletins earlier in the day because she couldn't concentrate on a single thing after Thad barreled out of her office. She felt awful about the way he had misinterpreted her hesitation. It was all she could think about.

Why had he turned on her so fast? It was almost like he'd been *waiting* for her to refuse him.

She wished she'd thought faster. Why hadn't she simply said yes? That was what she wanted to do, actually what she'd planned to do after she'd thought about it for a second. Unfortunately he'd misread the way she'd started to reply, and before she could correct his impression, he'd stomped out.

She'd just been so stunned. She hadn't expected him to ask her out, and she knew that through the thin, temporary walls of the new office her father was listening to every word they exchanged. And then, there was her past experience with Thad...

She hardly could believe he didn't remember her at all. But then again, she knew she wasn't particularly memorable. So why was he asking her out now?

And more important, why did she want to accept? He'd been the worst kind of cad the first time they'd met. But somehow he didn't seem remotely related to that man now. Beneath the bad boy he flaunted for the world was a vulnerable core—could everyone see it as clearly as she could?

Apparently not. Her father certainly didn't appear to notice what a nice man Thad could be. She recalled her father's words about Thad taking advantage of young women, and she wondered again what he had meant.

Her thoughts were drawn back to Thad, and she knew

indicated it was time to close the office. Rising from her desk, she gathered her things and locked up, heading for her car.

This time she knew where she was going.

It didn't take her long to get to the rusty trailer. Pulling into the drive, she noticed that Thad's rental truck was parked next to the trailer, rather than back near his workshop. Taking a deep breath, she walked across the grass to the door of the mobile home and rapped sharply on the metal screen.

The hum of a window air-conditioning unit masked any sound from inside. No one came to the door. She had almost convinced herself no one was home when the door swung inward and Thad stood before her.

He didn't speak, didn't open the screen that stood between them, merely surveyed her in a manner that gave nothing away.

"Hello." Her voice sounded calmer than she felt. "May I come in?"

Still without uttering a greeting, he reached out a hand and pushed open the screen, then stood back to let her pass inside. She was acutely aware of his big body only inches from her as she stepped into his home. When he closed the door behind her, she felt jittery and even more nervous than she had before. Vulnerable.

To avoid thinking further along those lines, she opened her mouth and rushed into the speech she had prepared on the drive out. "I came to tell you that you misinterpreted my words in the office this afternoon. After you asked me to dinner, I mean."

She waited a beat, but he didn't react in any way. She didn't know what she'd expected, but this wall of silence wasn't it.

"I was only thinking out loud when I started to answer you,'' she said. ''I wasn't going to refuse your invitation.''

He shrugged. ''Sorry I misunderstood. It's probably just as well—it was a lousy idea, anyway.'' He walked around her to the tiny kitchen area of the mobile home. ''Would you like a drink?''

''No, thank you.'' *Lousy idea for whom?* she wanted to ask, but insecurity and ingrained manners caught her tongue. He could only mean one thing, that he'd thought better of what she assumed had been an impulsive decision.

But if it had been impulse, then why had he driven past her office three times before he finally came in? Geiserville was a small town, and her office faced directly onto its main street. Did he think she hadn't noticed?

Thad scratched the back of his head. ''Well, would you like to sit down?''

''No, thank you.'' She wanted nothing more than to leave so she could finish being utterly humiliated in private. She'd come out here expecting to right the wrong between them, and anticipating...what? That they would make plans for a date, at the least.

She walked blindly to the door. ''I'll go now. I only wanted to clear up any misunderstanding.''

''Wait! Would you, uh, like the grand tour before you go?''

She turned and met his gaze, wondering why he wanted her to stick around when he didn't want to take her out.

He was smiling wryly as he indicated the postage-stamp dimensions of his living quarters. She wanted to refuse, to make him feel the way she was feeling, but when she opened her mouth to say no, she found that she couldn't deny herself an extra few moments of his company.

"All right."

"Step this way, madam." He grinned, and her breath hitched in her throat for a moment before she began to breathe again. It wasn't fair that he was so handsome, that her body felt more alive around him than it did around anyone she'd ever met.

She allowed him to usher her back through a tiny hallway. "I've never been in a trailer before. They're very...compact."

"Is that a nice way of saying tiny?" His voice was in her ear, and she knew that if she turned around they'd be face-to-face in the confines of the narrow hall. She didn't dare.

"This is interesting," she insisted. "Whoever designs these squeezed in a lot of living space. I've always wondered what they looked like inside."

"This is an old one. The newer models are probably much nicer." He indicated the bath with a sweep of his hand. "The powder room." And at the end of the short hall, if it could really be called that, he opened the single door. "My office—where I also sleep."

He wasn't kidding. Built-in shelves and a desk covered most of the space that wasn't taken up by a large bed in the corner. The shelves were covered with books, some fiction, she noticed in a quick survey, but others— many others—on various aspects of the art of woodworking. The bed was a light wood with a beautifully carved headboard that boasted high posts at each side. She noticed the desk was a similar design in the same wood.

"This is beautiful." She ran her hand over the satiny

surface of the desk in one place where it wasn't covered by papers. "Did you make these pieces?"

Thad nodded. "Thank you. I like working with oak."

Chloe smiled. "I wouldn't know oak from…"

"Mahogany?" he suggested.

"Exactly." She made a wry face. "Wood wasn't one of the things I studied in school."

"College, you mean?"

"Yes." She glanced up at him, wondering what he was thinking. She doubted that he had an advanced degree. In fact, she didn't even know for sure that he was a high school graduate. Still, intelligence shone from his blue eyes and she reminded herself that a lack of education didn't go hand in hand with ignorance.

"It takes a college degree to be a church secretary?"

He couldn't know how that stung, and she tried to keep the defensiveness from her tone when she answered. "It's supposed to be a temporary position until they replace the secretary who just retired. I'm trained to teach. I hope to open a preschool at the church for disadvantaged children." Reality intruded, and she murmured, "At least, I *did*."

Thad winced in sympathy. "It'll work out. I bet they'll have that church rebuilt within two years." Then he pointed at the papers that littered his desk. She had noticed more of the same mess on a small card table wedged into a corner of his living room alongside a single couch. "I'm really bad with the paperwork. You might not have been trained to do it, but it looks like you run that office with one hand tied behind your back." He grimaced. "I can't even find time to sit down and go through this mess. Or maybe—" he grinned sheepishly "—it's that I can't bring myself to."

"I could help you." She told herself that she had no

ulterior motives, that after the way he'd saved her, it was only right that she repay him in some way.

"No! I wasn't angling for help, honest." Thad looked slightly panicked at her offer.

"I know." She smiled calmly, though her insides felt anything but calm. "You saved my life. I'd be glad of the opportunity to repay you in some way. I could help you straighten out your books or type some letters or invoices...whatever it is you need me to do most."

The words fell between them, and immediately she realized that her words could be taken in more ways than one. Thad hadn't missed it, either, she was sure. A warm blue glow lit his eyes and though he didn't move a muscle, she felt as if he'd touched her. Her breath came faster, and her knees felt wobbly. She put out a hand to steady herself on the desk, but he took it before it made contact with the wooden surface.

How could she have thought she knew what it was like to be touched by him? Slowly he drew her close, and she could feel the energy running between their joined hands, the heat his body gave off. She held her breath, unwilling to disturb the intimacy of the moment even by breathing.

And then Thad released her hand and stepped back. "I would be very grateful for your help," he said, and his voice sounded hoarse and deeper than normal. "But I'll pay you. You're not doing it for free."

She would have argued with him, but she was too busy trying to keep her knees from dropping her to the floor. Inhaling deeply, she only nodded.

Thad moved ahead of her, back into the little living room. "The most urgent stuff is out here," he told her. "You tell me when you want to start, and I'll get it organized so you know what to do."

* * *

The elders met the following week and voted to hire Thad to help with the rebuilding of the church. He met with the architect in charge of the project and the building committee twice at the office. The second time, the group concluded its meeting just before lunch on Saturday.

Chloe was working in the outer office when the group filed out. She'd had some filing she'd wanted to get done, anyway, and since she'd had to come downtown and unlock the office, she decided to stay. Although she'd insisted to herself in the morning that that had been her only motive, she called herself a liar fifty times after Thad stepped out of the conference room and smiled at her. While she busied herself with needless paperwork and tried to pretend she was unaware of every move he made, he glanced over the table of old photographs of the church.

When she looked up again, he was standing beside her desk. "Are you finished?"

She nodded, acutely aware that the others had all gone out and they were alone in the office.

"Want to grab a bite to eat?" His voice was supremely casual.

Chloe nodded while her stomach did a mad dance. He had just asked her out again! "That would be nice."

As she got her purse and preceded him out the door before turning to lock it securely, she tried to gather her careening thoughts back into some semblance of normalcy. It was only lunch. He might just want to talk business. It wasn't really a date.

But they didn't talk business. Not church business or his office work.

Instead, he made small talk until the waitress in the

downtown diner had taken their order and then asked, "So tell me about the school you want to start."

She was surprised by his request, so much so that it took her a long moment to marshal her thoughts. It had been a long time since anyone had been interested in listening to her talk about her plans for a preschool. Her father so clearly *didn't* want to hear about it that she'd stopped even trying to explain all her ideas to him. With Thad, explanations were easy.

"My father means well," she said, trying to make Thad understand. "But he needed me to help him for a while, and I guess I made it too easy for him. He'll never look for another secretary unless I force the issue."

"So what's stopping you?" Thad sounded almost challenging. "It's one thing to respect your father, but it's another altogether to let him kill your dreams."

Kill her dreams... In a way, she supposed that was exactly what was happening. It was a shock to realize that she had almost convinced herself she would never have the chance to open a preschool.

"I had made up my mind to talk to him about it again," she said. "But then, after the explosion, I just didn't see how a new person could step into this mess. I've settled, I suppose, for waiting until the church is rebuilt."

"But that could be two years or more. You've got everything reorganized *now*. There's no reason a new person couldn't work with you for a month or so and then take over. True, you might need to do some fast talking to find a space and figure out some financing until your own church has a space for you, but you shouldn't wait."

He reached across the table and covered her right

hand with his own larger one. "I bet you'd be a great teacher. You shouldn't give up on your dreams."

She blushed. It wasn't a particularly intimate conversation, but his tone was low and seductive and his words made her feel as happy as if he'd told her she were a raving beauty. She hadn't had a champion *ever*, that she could recall.

"Do you have dreams?" She was curious. She knew so little about him, and it was suddenly important that he share some of himself the way she just had.

When he pulled his hand away and sat back abruptly, she felt like she'd been tossed into a cold lake. "My dreams all died a long time ago," he said in a tone that cautioned her not to cross the line.

"But aren't you doing what you want to do?" She thought he seemed happy with his work, fulfilled by the creative demands involved and satisfied to be doing it on his own terms.

To her surprise he relaxed again. "Yeah, I like my work. It's a good thing, too, since it's all I've ever been good at."

Then he glanced at his watch. "Speaking of which—I hate to cut this short, but I have some work waiting for me at home."

She rose, intending to pick up the bill and pay for her share, but he forestalled her effort. "I've got it."

Short of wrestling him for the tab, she didn't have a choice. "Thank you. Next time I'll treat."

He smiled, and she could have stood all day looking into those blue, blue eyes. "I'll hold you to that."

She smiled back, overly happy that he seemed ready to spend a "next time" with her, and went to the ladies' room while he paid.

As she came out of the stall, a heavy-set matron she

recognized as a clerk at the shoe store smiled and said hello. Then, without waiting for a response, the woman said, "I couldn't help but notice you had lunch with the Shippen boy. Better watch your step with that one, or you'll wind up in a bad way."

He's not a boy, he's all man, Chloe wanted to inform the woman. Even more, she wanted to know why everyone assumed the worst about him. But she did neither.

Another woman came in just in time to hear the first one's words. "You do know his mother *entertained men,*" she said with arched brows.

The first woman, delighted to have a sympathetic ear, volunteered, "Why, I hear she doesn't even know who that boy's father was."

Poor Thad. Chloe snapped her purse shut with unnecessary force. She still hadn't said a word, and the women were watching her. Well, they weren't going to have the pleasure of seeing if their words upset her. She stared back at the first woman, arching her eyebrow in a manner that conveyed silent disapproval. When the woman flushed and looked away, she turned the same stare on the second gossip, who stared back for less than five seconds before dropping her gaze to the hands she was waving under the dryer.

Chloe yanked open the door of the ladies'. No wonder Thad was so determined not to care what anyone thought. These people didn't even wait to hear the facts before spewing their nasty gossip across town.

Four

Okay, it probably was a little on the sneaky side, Thad decided, as he walked down the street toward Chloe's office on Monday a week later. Taking Chloe along to his appointment with the bank executive who could approve a line of credit for his business was a little like taking an apple to the teacher. He'd told Chloe it would be helpful to have her with him since she had helped him organize his books, but he knew her presence could only improve his chances for the loan.

He would feel bad about it if he didn't genuinely want her at his side.

She'd begun to accept him, he thought, since he'd adopted a lower-key approach. Oh, he still wanted her, and though he told himself again and again that she wasn't his kind of woman, he was drawn back to her day after day like a rabbit to a vegetable garden. He knew things were bad when he actually considered going to church just so he could see her on Sundays.

So far, he'd resisted such idiocy.

What he really wanted to do was to ask her out again. He told himself lunch didn't really count. He wanted to take her dancing. It was the only way he could think of to get her into his arms. But recalling the indecision that had clouded her eyes the first time he'd asked was enough to stop him. A man could only take so much rejection.

Yeah, she'd said she hadn't been going to refuse. Yet he didn't think he'd misread her—she might want to go out with him, but she was afraid of the idea.

Why? Okay, he knew she was...naive. His mind skirted around the V-word like it was a live grenade. He told himself he wasn't just interested in taking Chloe to bed, but his baser side stood up and laughed in his face. *So you don't want her in your bed? What are you dating her for, then? So you can join the church bingo club?*

A woman swept across the bank lobby, interrupting his mental wanderings. To his surprise she was smiling, though as she greeted Chloe and him he read the avid curiosity she was trying hard to mask.

Chloe was cheerful and sweet to the woman as she completely ignored the speculative glances. She was that nice to everyone they encountered, and it amused him no end. She could give a busybody absolutely no information and still make the person think they'd been awarded special treatment. He wondered how much she knew about his past, and if she'd give him the time of day if she learned about Jean.

Hell, maybe she already knew. He couldn't imagine that her old man hadn't shared all the sordid details.

Reverend Miller had handled Jean's funeral, though her family hadn't been big on church. He'd listened to the lies Jean's father had fed him and made up his mind about Thad, without once talking to *him*, the man who'd married her and whose child had died with her.

Abruptly he realized Chloe was speaking to him, and he forced his mind back to the present.

"We could go and get a pizza when we're done here…if you like."

He smiled down at her, liking the hesitancy with which she phrased her suggestion. "Yeah, that would be nice." Then a thought struck him and he smiled to himself. It was about time he had her to himself, even if it was only for a lunch hour. Excusing himself, he went to find a telephone.

The interview for a line of credit went more smoothly than Thad had expected. The banker was clearly surprised to see the summarized figures of his business, and his eyebrows rose when he saw the net profits. "Are you sure you even need this line, Mr. Shippen?"

Thad nodded, pleased and relieved at the man's professional attitude. "I want to buy a new piece of equipment that would allow me to try some new things, expand the kinds of restoration I can do right now."

The banker frowned, and Thad braced himself. "You might be better off with a straight-forward loan. The rate of interest would be better, and you would have a longer time to pay it off."

Anxiety disappeared again and he relaxed. "That would be nice, but unfortunately I need the line because I'm frequently forced to buy materials at the beginning of a job…and of course, I don't get paid until the end."

The banker nodded again. "Yes, I see…" He reached for a calculator and rapidly punched in several sets of numbers. When he looked up, he was smiling. "I believe that if you're interested, we could extend you both offers, a line of credit and the lower-interest loan."

It took a moment for the words to sink in.

Chloe turned to look at him. "That makes good sense, Thad. I think you should do it that way."

"Of course I'll need to visit your workshop, see your operation," the banker said. "But I don't anticipate that will be any problem. You have a reputation for doing good work at fair prices. Besides, you have the collateral, and your credit history is excellent."

He didn't know what to say. No one had ever extended a single extra crumb of advice or trust to him in the past, in this bank or the other one down the street. He was convinced it was Chloe's presence. It had to be.

A quarter hour later, they were climbing into his truck. He had an appointment to show the banker his workshop next week and completed copies of his loan applications in his hand.

"I can't believe it!" he exulted as he pulled into traffic. "That was great!"

"It did go well," Chloe was smiling, and he reached over and grabbed her hand, squeezing it tightly.

"Thank you."

"I didn't do anything," she protested.

"You prepared the information for me," he countered. "And you went with me." He pressed the back of her hand to his lips and smacked a lavish kiss onto it. "My good-luck charm."

She shook her head. "That's silly. Whether or not I helped, you still have the figures to show your business is solid."

He flashed her a grin, pleased that she hadn't pulled her hand away. Her skin was incredibly silky and soft, and he rubbed his thumb lightly over the back of her hand, reveling in the tactile pleasure. "You're my good-luck charm," he repeated as he swung the truck into the parking lot of the pizza place.

Chloe reached for her door handle, but he forestalled her move. "We're not going in."

"We're not?"

"Nope." He squeezed her hand once more, then released it. "Wait right here. I'll be back."

The silence was too sudden, too *loud,* in a funny way, when he cut the engine outside his trailer. She'd known since he'd reappeared with the pizza in a box to go that they were coming here, to his trailer. She felt jumpy, nervous with anticipation...which was silly when he hadn't indicated that there was anything more to this than lunch in a quiet spot.

Still, she knew that when the door of that tiny trailer closed behind them, she was going to be a nervous wreck. She was terrible at small talk. And when she was nervous, she was worse than terrible—her mind dried up like a shallow stream in a drought.

While she'd been thinking these morose thoughts, Thad had gotten out of the truck. Balancing the pizza in one hand, he came around and opened her door.

"Thank you," she said.

"Don't sound so surprised." His voice was dry. "I am capable of manners."

"I didn't mean—you're not—it wasn't meant as an insult."

"I didn't take it as one," he said, grinning. Then, as she watched in puzzlement, he walked around to the back of the trailer. "Come on—I'll get a blanket and we'll eat back here."

Behind the trailer was a small square of mowed lawn, shaded by the big trees that surrounded his home. The day was warm and the season early enough that insects weren't a nuisance yet. It was a perfectly lovely place for a picnic lunch, with flowering shrubs that surrounded the trailer displaying their blooms and wild daffodils and bluebells dancing around the fringes of the yard. Thad unlocked the back door to the trailer and took out a blanket, which he spread on the grass with a flourish.

"Please take a seat." When he offered her his hand she accepted it with a smile, bemused by his sudden whimsical manner. After escorting her to a seat on the blanket, he went back inside and returned again, with paper plates and napkins, two plastic cups and a bottle of wine which he had uncorked.

Chloe eyed the wine. Should she tell him she didn't drink? In fact, that she'd never even drunk wine other than the minuscule sip of communion wine? No, probably not necessary. After all, this was lunch. How drunk could a person get from a glass of wine with a meal? People did it all the time.

As Thad settled on the blanket beside her, her nervousness returned. "This is lovely," she said, indicating the flowers all around them. "I love spring because so many pretty things are blooming."

He nodded. "It is nice. I don't usually stop to appreciate it. All this was here when I bought it. I just try to keep the weeds in check and the trees and bushes trimmed when I get a chance."

He opened the pizza box and slid a slice onto her plate, then poured her a cup of the wine. It was a clear, pale gold and she sipped it experimentally. Hmm...not bad. It wasn't as sickeningly sweet as the communion wine. She took a bigger sip. "So when did you buy this place?"

Thad squinted his eyes in thought as he chewed. "Let's see—I guess it's been about three years. I grew up around here, but I moved away about a year after I got out of high school. I hadn't planned on ever coming back, but when my mother told me she was sick, I decided I needed to be closer."

Three years... With a small shock, she realized he must have come back right around the time she'd met him at that party. To cover her reaction, she picked up her cup and drank again.

"My mother would never ask me for help," Thad went on. "But I know she needs me. She's having more trouble getting around, and she needs help with laundry and the garbage, things like that." He swirled the wine in his cup. "I guess you've heard that my mother isn't exactly the perfect lady, but she doesn't deserve this."

"Nobody deserves it," Chloe said. "God doesn't pick and choose who's going to get ill based on the way they've lived their lives."

"The thing is, she's good-hearted," Thad said. He wasn't looking at her, but down at his food. It was almost as if he were talking to himself. "Despite her flaws, she's one of the nicest people you'll ever meet."

"I'd like to meet her," Chloe said gently. "She sounds like a very nice lady. My father enjoyed his visit with her."

"My mother enjoyed talking to him, too." Thad looked over at her. "Why did he go, anyway? Your father has never gone out of his way to do me any favors. It's easier to dislike him when he acts like a jerk all the time."

Chloe took another sip of her wine. It certainly was

a glorious day and she refused to take offense at his words. "My father is human, just like the rest of us, and certainly not perfect." She cast him a steady look. "But he surely does seem to have you pegged as a villain. Why is that, Thad?"

Thad shrugged. "Who knows? Half this community feels the same."

Silence fell as they finished their meal. Thad poured more wine into her cup. She wasn't sure she needed any more—she felt a little light-headed already. The day was warm—a harbinger of summer to come. Birds whistled and sang in the trees. There wasn't another soul around and the little garden felt intimate and cozy. Thad had stretched out his legs and was leaning back on his hands with his face tilted up to the sun.

"My father called you a defiler of young women. Why?" Good heavens, what a thing to ask a person! Chloe set her cup firmly aside. No more of that if it loosened her tongue and her mind like this. The question was intrusive, insulting. "Never mind," she said hurriedly. "It's none of my business—"

"Yes, it is." With three simple words, he changed the nature of their relationship. "It's only fair that you know what kind of man I am. You might not want to keep on seeing me."

She couldn't look at him, so she studied the blanket instead. No power on earth was going to take away her desire to be with him. But she wasn't about to tell him that.

He turned his head and looked at her, and she read bleak self-hate in his eyes. "I got a girl pregnant right before I graduated from high school. Her name was Jean—she was in my class in school but she wasn't the kind of girl I usually went out with. Jean was a *nice* girl.''

She waited, but he didn't speak more. She wondered what he was thinking, and decided he was probably waiting for her to express her horror. "Poor girl,'' she said in a mild tone. "I think finding out you're expecting a baby out of wedlock is probably a frightening experience for any young girl.''

"Her family threw her out when we told them about the baby.''

Chloe gasped. "That's terrible!'' How could anyone do that to their own child?

"I thought so. Anyway, we moved in with my mother. You can imagine what people thought of *that*. My mother wasn't happy about the situation, either, but she was good to Jean. As soon as we graduated, we got married.'' He stopped for a moment, and Chloe was grateful for the pause.

Her world had just turned upside down. *He'd been married*. Somehow, she'd never considered that, and she didn't like the way it made her feel inside. Jealous and possessive, even though there wasn't a shred of doubt in her mind that he wasn't married now. Thad wouldn't do that—take her, Chloe, out to lunch if he had a wife somewhere.

She realized he was watching her.

"What are you thinking?'' he asked.

"What happened to your marriage?''

He didn't bat an eyelash. "Maybe I'm still married.''

She tried a smile, but her lips quivered and she abandoned the effort. "You're not that kind of man. If you were still married, you'd be sitting here on this blanket with your wife.''

"Why do you have such faith in me?" He was watching her intently.

She shrugged, twisting her fingers into a pretzel. "You're a good person."

Thad snorted. "There aren't a lot of people who would agree with you."

"Yes, there are." She did look at him then, annoyed at the way he always managed to put himself down. "That banker thinks you're a good person, doesn't he? Your trouble is, you're so determined not to give people a chance to slight you that you assume they're all the same. Yes, there are vicious gossips and judgmental individuals in this town, but there also are a lot of nice people who would befriend you if you'd stop looking for insults at every turn."

She stopped for breath. "So quit the self-condemnation. You were a young man who got into a situation all too common to young people. Lots of young people fall in love and—"

"But that's just it."

"Just what?"

"It wasn't love. At least, not for me." His face twisted. "That's the worst part of it. I wish I had loved her. God, I wanted to. Jean never made any secret of the way she felt, but I—if there hadn't been a baby on the way, I wouldn't have made any permanent plans for the relationship."

"You mean it would have been just another one-night stand."

He exhaled deeply. "Yeah, I guess that about sums it up." He turned his head, and his eyes swept over her briefly. "I told you I'm not a very nice guy."

"Would you—" She stopped, trying to choose just

the right words. "Are one-night stands still a common thing for you?"

Startled, he sat bolt upright and glared at her. "Of course not."

She smiled at his indignation. "Why?"

"Because I'm ashamed! Because it's wrong to treat women like disposable items, used once and tossed out. Oh. You think you're smart." He gave her a wry smile. "You're determined to make me a nicer guy, aren't you?"

"Not really. Just determined, maybe, to make you see you're not as despicable as you think you are. Everybody makes mistakes."

"Maybe," he muttered. "But some are a lot bigger than others."

Again they didn't speak for a few moments. Then she stirred, taking in the details of his profile, washed in a bath of strong white light. "You've managed to distract me. Finish the story."

Thad kept his face turned up to the sun. "There's not much more to tell. Jean was diabetic. I didn't know. She hid it from me." He jackknifed into a sitting position, his face contorted in pain. "If I'd known—" His voice cracked as he went on. "We didn't have much money so Jean didn't go to the doctor. She said there was no reason, that we'd need the money more when the baby came. One day I found her on our bed, unconscious. I didn't realize it, but she was in a diabetic coma."

He paused, and when he continued, his voice was flat and expressionless. "Jean never woke up. She died that night, and even though they tried a Caesarean section to save the baby, our little boy died, too. Jean's family blames me for killing her. And I did. A woman with her medical condition... She'd been told never to have children, that pregnancy could be fatal.''

"You can't believe that." Chloe reached for his fisted hands, wrapping her own over his knuckles and squeezing. "How would you have known if Jean didn't tell you? Are you a mind reader?"

"I should have known something was wrong," he muttered. "She always kept crackers in her purse, was always getting light-headed... I should have figured it out."

"Those are common behaviors for pregnant ladies," she pointed out. "How well did you know her before you...before she—" She stopped, not quite able to utter the words.

"We went out three times," he said. "I told you— it wasn't a long-term relationship, at least in my mind, until she turned up pregnant."

"So you didn't really know her habits well enough to suspect she had an illness. She *chose* to hide it from you, Thad. She must have had reasons for that."

He sighed heavily, looking away from her. "Jean wasn't very secure about our relationship. I think she was afraid I wouldn't want her if I found out." He looked at her and she could see the anguish in his eyes. "I wouldn't have left my child fatherless...ever."

"I know you wouldn't," she said softly. "But I imagine she wasn't thinking very clearly."

"I think she was embarrassed, too. She told me once that it's hard to be different when you're a teenager. At the time, I brushed it off because I couldn't see that she'd been anywhere near as 'different' as I was. Now it's easy to see she was talking about her disease."

Chloe smoothed her thumbs across the backs of his hands. "What happened is sad and tragic, but it wasn't your fault. Her family probably just made you the target for their grief."

"They did a great job of hitting the bull's-eye." His tone was laced with pain. "The thing I can never forgive myself for is never telling her I loved her. She was always so open, so affectionate and giving—"

"I'm sure she believed you loved her." She kept her voice low and soothing.

"God, I hope so." His shoulders slumped. "I was never big on praying, but after she died, I prayed that she never knew the only reason I married her was because I didn't want my kid to grow up never knowing his father."

Like I did.

He didn't have to say the words. They whispered insistently in the air between them.

She scooted across the blanket without stopping to think, putting her arms around his broad shoulders. His leg was pressed against hers as they knelt, face-to-face, and she put a hand to the side of his face and stroked gently. "You know what I think? I think God forgave you for all these wrongs you've stacked up in your head. You need to forgive yourself."

Thad shuddered, his hand coming up to cover hers in a convulsive, desperate grip. "You're good for me."

She smiled at him, her lips trembling despite her best efforts. His story touched her deeply, and she was determined to release him of his burden of guilt. Trying to lighten the intensity of the moment, she smiled softly at him. "You make me sound like chicken broth."

One golden eyebrow rose and she saw his shoulders relax, the corners of his mouth lift. "You don't look like chicken broth."

She returned his smile, lifting her gaze to his. Their

eyes met, clung for a long moment...a moment in which she could almost feel the sparks of attraction flying between them, like static in her hair when it was freshly washed.

"Do you taste like chicken broth?" he whispered. Their faces were so close she could feel the sweet warmth of his breath against her face. It never occurred to her to be alarmed. As he lowered his mouth to hers she closed her eyes, holding her breath in unconscious anticipation.

Then his mouth closed over hers, a soft, tender pressure. Immediately her hand slipped from the side of his face to his strong neck, and she sank against him, spellbound by the sweetness of the intimacy. His mouth left hers then, and without fully realizing the significance of her action, she tightened her arm around his neck to prolong the contact.

He hesitated for a moment, holding himself stiffly away from her, but as she continued to press her mouth against his, seeking more of his kisses, he slipped his arms around her and angled his mouth over hers.

His kiss was no longer soft, but hard and demanding, and she responded with every fiber of her being. This was what—*who*—she'd been made for, she thought in dizzy pleasure. Tilting her face more fully to his, she lay against him, overwhelmed by sensation. Her breath came in shallow gulps as her sensitive breasts were flattened against his broad chest. Arrows of unfamiliar sensation shot straight down to center at the very bottom of her torso, and she let him gather her even closer, seeking more of the strange delight. His tongue traced the seam of her closed lips, then probed gently, and she opened her mouth to admit him. Instantly he took advantage of the yielding, exploring her mouth with thorough strokes of his tongue. She moaned again and slid one hand up to clench his hair as the other wound around his neck.

Holding her tightly to him, Thad pressed her backward. She slipped her legs to one side as his weight came down across her, and she tightened her arms around him. This was what she wanted, what she needed. She was a creature of response, his to mold and shape as he willed. His kisses stoked the blaze within her until she was moaning beneath him, seeking more with restless movements of her hips.

"Thad," she said against his mouth, and his name segued into a groan of pleasure as he shifted his legs to lie fully atop her. Her body knew this man's weight, recognized his hard, muscular strength and urged her to assuage the yearning he aroused. Her hips lifted, rolling rhythmically beneath him, but as she laced her arms around his shoulders more tightly she felt his body tense over hers.

With a sudden, violent curse that scorched her ears, he rolled away from her and surged to his feet, standing with his back to her, one hand on his hip and the other gripping the back of his neck. Her body throbbed with an insistent ache and just as suddenly as he had moved, a clear image of her own abandoned behavior coalesced in her mind.

God forgive her, what was she doing?

A blinding shame rose within her as she sat up, then climbed to her feet and straightened her clothes with fingers that trembled.

She, who had always prided herself on her good sense and her ability to overcome temptations, had succumbed—no, not succumbed, she acknowledged—had invited intimate foreplay from a man. *Not just any man,* her heart insisted. *Thad.*

It didn't matter who the man was, she told herself sternly. What mattered was that if *he* hadn't stopped it, she would have let him touch, taste, take her in the most basic way a man and a woman could unite. A way that she'd always believed was meaningless without a commitment of the heart, a commitment sealed by the bonds of matrimony.

Her whole face felt hot with self-loathing and embarrassment as she reached for her purse and looked wildly around. Her car...where had she parked her car?

Then she remembered. She hadn't. Her heart sank as she realized she was dependent on Thad for a ride. She dashed tears of frustration away with an ungentle swipe of her hand as he turned to face her.

"Chloe, I didn't—are you crying?" he demanded, striding across the grass. He put his hands to her waist, and she was appalled at her treacherous body's urge to turn into his arms again.

She made herself still and stiff under his hands. "Could you please take me back to my car? I'm sorry if I led you to believe that I—that we—oh, never mind! May we please leave?"

"No."

Shocked out of her racing thoughts, she stared up at him. "I beg your pardon?"

A grim smile touched the corners of his mouth as he released her. "You can beg all you like, honey, but we're not leaving here until we've talked about what just happened."

Ohh, what she wouldn't give for the power to snap her fingers and make him disappear. "What just happened," she said through clenched teeth, "was that I nearly threw away a whole lifetime of beliefs. And if you hadn't stopped, I never would have thought to stop you. I am totally humiliated and painfully aware of my failure. Is that what you want to hear?''

"Not exactly," Thad said. There was a warm light in his eyes that she couldn't decipher. "So I'm not wrong in thinking you liked it?"

"I don't tell lies," she said steadily, looking past him at the flowers along the edge of the grassy spot.

"Do you want to hear my take on this?" he asked, and waited until she had raised her gaze to his. "What happened to me was that you turned me on so quickly and so completely that I nearly forgot how much I like and respect you. There's no reason for you to feel humiliated."

"No reason? Did you hear me calling a halt? I barely remembered my name, much less my principles." Her tone was bitter.

"If anything, I'm the one who should feel bad," he went on. "I'm not a teenager who thinks with his glands anymore. I've had firsthand experience with the consequences of reckless sex. I know better."

"You don't have to feel bad. You stopped, remember?"

Thad grinned. "You sound like you're sorry." He took her hands again, and upset as she was, she couldn't bring herself to pull away. Just the touch of his thumbs rubbing across the back of her knuckles made her knees weaken anew. "What happened between us was perfectly normal for two people who are attracted to each other. Taking my hands off you has to be the toughest thing I've ever done in my life."

She tried to hold on to her outrage, even to her pique, but somewhere inside she was pleased to know that it hadn't been easy for him, either. The humor of having a discussion like this while standing in his backyard began to dawn on her and she slanted him a teasing smile. "And the noblest, too, no doubt."

"No doubt." His tone was heartfelt. Their eyes made contact for a long moment, then Thad dropped her hands. She actually could see him distancing himself from her before he spoke again. "Chloe, I'm very attracted to you. But I also enjoy being with you more than any woman I can remember. I'd like to see you again."

His gaze was earnest and his voice was sincere. Her heart skipped a beat, then returned to a rhythm twice its normal speed. She knew she would have to be insane to go out with him again, after what had almost happened here today. He definitely wasn't the kind of man she should be involved with. If she were smart, she'd get out of here fast and never see him again.

"I'd like that, too."

"Good." He leaned forward and pressed a quick kiss to her lips before she could dodge or respond, then turned away to gather up the picnic things. "Now I'm getting you out of here before my willpower deserts me altogether."

Five

The next day was Sunday. Thad had asked her to take a walk on the Appalachian Trail in the afternoon, and Chloe accepted, knowing her father would be having lunch with one of the parishioners, and that lunch would probably stretch well into the afternoon. She daydreamed through the church service, then watched the clock like a hawk all through lunch. A minute wasn't really that long, was it?

Finally, just as one o'clock arrived, the doorbell rang. The butterflies in her stomach lifted off in a great cloud of fluttering wings. She half ran to the door, then took a deep breath before she put her hand on the knob. *Chloe Miller, this is just a date, not your wedding day! Settle down.*

Thad was standing on the porch when she pulled the door open. He was smiling, and she smiled back, struck by how handsome he was. He wore a forest green T-shirt and blue jeans, and in contrast to the green of the shirt, his eyes blazed more beautifully blue than ever. She was aware of every inch of his tall, hard body, though she had yet to look away from his eyes, and the butterflies in her stomach winged their way to a lower spot, bringing her body to throbbing life.

"Ready for a stroll?"

She watched his lips form the words and longed to press her own to his, to feel his mobile mouth move as he formed the words. The lips curved up into a smile that spread to reveal strong white teeth. He chuckled.

With a start she realized an answer was required, and that undoubtedly he knew exactly what was going through her head.

She could feel the heat in her cheeks as she turned away. "Let me get my jacket."

After retrieving her lightweight coat, she locked the door behind her, and Thad escorted her to his now-familiar truck. He headed for the Blue Ridge Mountains, where they would pick up the trail.

It was a warm, sunny, spring day. The section of the Appalachian Trail they walked along wound through forest and wandered past rushing streams filled with the remnants of melted winter. New buds studded all the vegetation within sight, though without the shade of summer's leafy canopy, the May sun was surprisingly hot. Chloe took off her jacket and tied the sleeves around her shoulders. Thad did the same with the sweatshirt he'd donned before they'd begun to walk, but anchored it around his lean waist.

As they strolled over the well-marked path, he asked her questions about the financial aspects of setting up for a preschool. He was easy to confide in, and she thrilled to the delight of sharing her ideas with someone who was genuinely interested. He made suggestions occasionally and asked questions that she found she had to consider carefully. Before she knew it, thirty minutes had passed.

"Let's take a break before we start back," he suggested, pointing to a large boulder with a flat plateau on one side that leaned drunkenly a few yards off the trail.

"Sounds good. I didn't realize how pitifully out of shape I am," she confessed. The hike had been a slight uphill incline and she was breathing fast.

White teeth flashed in a quick smile. "Here's my cue to tell you what I think of your shape."

She clucked her tongue at him. "Behave."

He heaved an exaggerated sigh behind her.

"Let me check for snakes," he suggested as she clambered up onto the lichened stone surface.

"Snakes?" She froze, one leg dangling.

"There are copperheads in these hills. On a day like this, they might be taking a nap on a nice, warm rock like this."

She launched herself away from the rough gray of the boulder's face, landing less than gracefully on the ground beside him. "Don't let me stop you."

He laughed aloud as he hoisted himself up and stomped around atop the rock. "Okay."

She took his offered hand and perched gingerly on the stone, peering around her. "I don't know much about snakes. You don't think they'd come up while we're here, do you?"

He settled beside her, resting his elbows on his drawn-up knees. "Doubt it. Snakes would rather run than fight. If you give them plenty of warning, they generally leave you alone."

"How do you know all this?"

A rueful smile touched his lips. "When I was a teen-ager, these mountains were a great place to come for parties. There are so many little roads and tracks and hidden spots that we rarely got caught. I learned a long time ago that if I wanted to get a girl to relax, I'd better make sure there were no snakes around."

"So bringing girls up here to...relax, was a frequent occurrence?"

"Not that frequent." He shot her a smug smile. "Jealous?"

"No! Just wondering how many other girls you picked up that you don't remember anymore."

As soon as she uttered the words, she was sorry. She could feel an instant rush of heat surging up her neck, and she dropped her head onto her raised knees. She could almost feel his gaze on her, and she knew there was no getting out of this now.

"Other girls?" His tone was low, quiet. Menacing. "Do you have a specific girl in mind that I'm supposed to have 'picked up'?"

She took a deep breath, feeling her breasts flatten against her knees. Without raising her head, she said, "Forget it. It was a stupid thing to say."

"No, I don't think I want to forget it." His voice was harder than she'd ever heard it, and she concentrated on making herself invisible. She wondered how long it would be before anyone found her body if he strangled her and threw her off a cliff up here somewhere.

"Dammit, Chloe! You can't just make an accusation like that and then zone out. What other girls are you talking about?"

With her head still on her knees, she muttered, "Me."

"Huh?"

As reactions went, it was a bit of a dud. "I'm talking about me," she said again, lifting her head.

He was completely mystified, and it showed in his voice. "What are you talking about? When did I ever forget you?" He shifted his body toward her, forcing her to put her hands on the rock behind her to keep from falling backward. Placing a hand on either side of her, he neatly boxed her in. "Believe me, I've never thought about a woman as much as I think about you."

Her heart gave an involuntary jolt.

"So," he went on, leaning even closer. "Explain."

She could barely breathe. His face was so close she could see the splinters of gold that fractured the blue of his eyes. She averted her face, withdrawing from him in the only way left to her. "We met before. Three years ago. It was August, at a party on Frey Street. I never did find out whose home it was."

"You expect me to believe you were at a keg party? If you're talking about the party I think you are, there were more illegal substances there than there were people to try 'em. Hardly your scene."

"It wasn't. Normally. I had had…a disagreement with my father and I was feeling rebellious, I guess. I came with a friend from high school. Margie Eadams. Maybe you know her? Well, she was really more of an acquaintance. We hadn't known each other well, and I don't know what possessed me to—"

"So how did we meet?"

"Oh. Well, I was sort of out of my league, if you want to know the truth—"

"No!"

She glared at him. "Do you want to hear this or not?"

"Oh, yeah, I want to hear it. Every detail. Go on."

"I was standing alone, trying to figure out how to get home—Margie had driven and she'd disappeared—and you came over and started talking. You took me outside and we sat on the back steps and talked."

When she stopped, he prompted, "And?"

She took a deep breath. "And then you touched me." Her voice was barely audible, her cheeks flushing a deeper rose with every passing moment.

"I touched you," he repeated slowly. "Where did I touch you, Chloe?"

"You touched...you touched my breast."

She heard him inhale sharply, but he didn't speak. When a few moments had passed and he still didn't say anything, she risked a glance at him. His features were drawn into a dark scowl. "Did I hurt you?"

She wasn't prepared for the question. "No. I mean, you startled me—a lot. I got up and walked away, and then I walked home."

That got his attention. "You walked home from Frey Street? That was a crazy thing to do at that time of night."

"Well, I wasn't about to hang around at that party any longer!"

"No, I guess not." He grimaced and exhaled deeply, his shoulders slumping. "I don't quite know what to say, except that I'm sorry. I don't remember much of that night. It wasn't one of the better days of my life. If it's any consolation to you, that was the last wild party I went to. I had just come back to town that day and I knew if I wanted people to take me seriously as a businessman, I couldn't slide back into that lifestyle."

"So the first thing you did was find a party?"

"Yeah." He uttered a short bark of laughter but there

was little humor in it. "I wasn't planning on ever coming back to this town. It seemed like a good idea to start fresh somewhere that people didn't know me. But my mother had just told me she was terminally ill, and I wanted to be there for her when she needed me. On top of that, when I was coming out of the hardware store the same day, I ran into—and I mean literally—Jean's mother. She was as surprised to see me as I was to see her. I said hello, hoping that maybe the years had helped her get over Jean's death, but she was just as loving as ever." He spoke the words in a measured, detached way that told her how hard he tried to pretend it didn't matter. "She called me a murderer and said some other complimentary things that anyone within earshot could hear." He rolled his shoulders as if he were stiff. "My sole ambition at that party that night was to get drunk enough to forget."

He half turned toward her. "I've changed since then, Chloe. Grown up, I guess. I never have more than two drinks anymore. I hated waking up the next day and not being able to remember anything." Then he cast her a small smile that mocked himself. "Now I'm even sorrier."

She could still feel herself blushing, but she forced herself to make normal conversation. "That sounds like a pretty terrible day. My method might have been different, but I would have wanted to forget it, too."

They sat for a moment longer without speaking. Then she stirred herself. "We'd better start back. I have to think about getting some dinner ready."

Thad stood and stretched, then leaped down from the boulder with the easy grace of a big mountain lion. He turned and extended a hand to her. Taking his hand, she slipped off the rock beside him and they started down the trail. He held her hand the whole way back to the truck, where he opened her door and helped her in.

When they arrived back at her house, he didn't shut off the engine, but got out and walked around to open her door. She stepped out of the truck, but he didn't move. Their bodies brushed, and suddenly, between the space of one heartbeat and the next, she was painfully aware of his body, of the way her nipples grew taut and her lower body softened and throbbed. He slid his arms around her waist and drew her against him. She gasped and he groaned as their bodies slid into perfect alignment.

"Thanks for going with me today." His voice was little more than a growl.

"You're welcome. I enjoyed it." She swallowed, and his eyes followed the motion of her throat. "I have to go in now."

"Okay." His lips hovered, descended, and she rose on tiptoe to meet his mouth, knowing only that she had to kiss him or die. This time she welcomed the thrust of his tongue and the way his hips mimicked the seduction of her mouth. She welcomed the hard press of his chest against her breasts and the way, lower down, that his body pushed at hers, giving her a restless, waiting feeling that went along with the softening she could feel happening to herself.

He kissed her and kissed her, right there in plain sight in front of her house, and she kissed him back. Finally Thad tore his mouth from hers and cradled the back of her skull in his palm, pressing her face into his shoulder. His hips, as if they were unconnected to the part of him that was stopping, thrust heavily against her, retreated, and then repeated the action twice more. Taking her by the shoulders, he set her a step away from him.

Chloe stood passively before him. What now? She needed more. She needed his tongue and his hands stroking her all over. She needed him. She reached for him, but he grabbed her wrists and held her hands securely between them.

"Chloe."

She blinked, looking up at him.

"Go inside. I'll see you tomorrow." He turned her around and gave her a push in the direction of the front door.

She took a step, then one more before she turned sluggishly, feeling like all her limbs were so heavy she could just lie down and take a nap on the spot. No, that was wrong. She did want to lie down, but she wanted Thad to lie down with her. On her. She wanted more of this wonderful silky, slippery slowness that had seized her.

But Thad wasn't there. As soon as he'd set her away, he'd started back to his truck. He was just climbing in the door and she focused hard, willing him to come back.

He started the engine. Then, with a wave that was barely a flip of his hand, he was gone.

Monday wasn't too busy, as Mondays were prone to be. It was a good thing, too, she decided, because in the state she was, she'd be lucky to get any work done at all. All she had to do was think of Thad and her body began jumping in anticipation, all her nerve endings quivering and throbbing. And that was all she *could* do—think of Thad.

That wasn't a good sign. She was glad he'd stopped when he did yesterday—wasn't she?—because it seemed to her that all he had to do was put his hand on her, and all her common sense flew right out the window. He was a good man, an honorable man. He didn't take advantage, even though it had to have been plain that he could have done anything he wanted with her. To her. The thought brought a delicious shiver with it.

People really didn't know him at all. He had done the right thing by the girl he'd gotten pregnant when he could have walked away. He was determined to build himself a successful business, and he was going about it the right way, getting a reputation for good work and fair prices despite the things some people thought about his character. He was a vulnerable soul, still agonizing, still shouldering guilt and blame for a sad accident that he hadn't known could happen. He *was* a good man, and she didn't care what anyone else thought. She saw the real Thad...and she loved him.

She loved him. The mere idea still made her breathless. She'd had all night to think, after he'd left her standing in front of the house, and she'd finally realized what she was feeling. She was pretty sure it wasn't just sexual attraction, although that was certainly wrapped up in it. It was love.

She didn't know how or when it had happened. She did know it was one-sided, and she experienced a sudden flare of empathy for poor Jean, who'd also loved him without being loved in return.

Unfortunately, Chloe would love him until the day she died, just like Jean. That subdued the pleasurable feelings considerably. She'd always assumed the love of her life would be reciprocated, that they'd marry and settle into doing the family thing, always conscious of their love for each other.

Now that idea had been blown right out of existence. Maybe one day, she would find a man who loved her, a man she cared for and could be a wife to, a man who might never know his wife carried in her heart the image of another man.

Her hands stilled on the papers she was halfheartedly trying to organize. It was going to be hard, walking away from the perfect ecstasy she knew she would find in Thad's arms. She was going to have to be very strong. She might not be able to bring wholehearted love to her future husband, but she was determined to come chaste, unused, so that he would always know he was the only one. It didn't matter that a tiny part of her didn't care a bit about virginity, couldn't wait to give it away. She wasn't doing *it* with anyone she wasn't married to. It just wouldn't be right for her.

Unfortunately the thought of the faceless, nameless husband was mildly revolting. She couldn't imagine any other hands but Thad's on her, couldn't imagine thrilling to anyone else's touch. Maybe she'd never marry. That might be the best thing. Oh, who knew?

The only thing she did know was that she wasn't going to see Thad again. Well, she might see him around town, but she wasn't going out with him again. It would hurt too much. Besides, she knew her limitations. If he really tried, he could have her in his bed—or have her anywhere else, for that matter—and she'd never utter a peep of protest. In fact, she'd be the one turning down the sheets. No, she couldn't take that chance.

She had stopped filing altogether and was just sitting with her hands on her desk when the door opened. Expecting her father back from an errand, she looked up with a smile pasted on her mouth—and froze.

It was Thad.

A slow smile curled the corners of his mouth as he

came through the door. "Good morning. I'm relieved to see you. Thought maybe you were still standing where I left you yesterday."

She could feel her face burning at the reminder of why she had been standing there. Could she never have a conversation with him without blushing? "Good morning."

He grinned. "You have your prim-and-proper face on. That turns me on, knowing I can make you look…less prim and proper." While his tone was teasing, his eyes were intent as he watched her.

"Did you come in for a reason?" She strove for a casual note. She wasn't going to let him affect her anymore.

"Yeah. I have to go down to the lumberyard and on my way back I'd like to take you out for lunch."

"I…I can't. I have too much work to do. I'm eating in the office today."

"Did you bring lunch?"

He knew she'd made it up. She could tell by the gleam in his eye. The doorbell jangled as one of the church members opened the door to the office. The phrase "saved by the bell" would have a whole new meaning for her after this.

"Good morning, Mrs. Fitzworth."

"Good morning, dear. Here are the minutes from last week's Missions meeting." The older woman shifted and smiled at Thad. "Good morning, Mr. Shippen. I understand you do woodwork repair."

"Yes, ma'am."

"Good. I have some wainscoting that was damaged by the previous owners of my home. Perhaps you'd like to look at it and give me an estimate?"

"I'd be happy to do that." Thad held the door open,

ushering her out. He gave Chloe a casual wave as he went down the steps, head cocked to listen to Mrs. Fitzworth's chatter.

She watched them as long as she could without getting up and pressing her nose against the glass window. Well. She wasn't sure what she'd expected, but having Thad accept her lie at face value and waltz out the door like he didn't even care—

Wasn't that what she wanted? Him out of her life? She should be happy, relieved, jumping up and down, joyous.

So why did she feel like a child who'd been scolded by her favorite teacher? Even though Thad was the farthest thing from a teacher she could imagine. She *had* to stop thinking about him! Resolutely, she applied herself to the paperwork in front of her, ignoring her growling stomach and the clock on the wall as it ticked past noon and on into the next hour. Her father returned from his hospital visits and several parishioners came and went. Every time that stupid bell over the door jangled, her heart hopped and she held her breath. But it was never Thad.

She was back at the copier when the bell sang its discordant notes again. "I'll be with you in a moment," she called, checking the tray to be sure it had plenty of paper. When she turned around, there he was. She could no sooner stop the silly smile she felt spreading across her face than she could the sun from rising as he held up a white bag.

"Since you're too busy to go out, I brought lunch in. If you haven't already eaten?"

"No, I haven't. Thank you," she added belatedly. What was the harm in sharing a sandwich with him?

They were in a very public place. She was in no danger of forgetting her principles here.

He pulled a chair up across from her at the desk, and she hastily moved a bud vase, her paperweight and a stack of files. "You're good for my image."

Startled, she glanced at him as he unwrapped a ham sandwich and another of chicken and indicated she should choose one. "What?"

"You're good for my image." He pulled two cans of soda from the bag and efficiently popped them open. "Mrs. Fitzworth just hired me for her job."

"That had nothing to do with me," she said briskly. "You're a fine person. People just need a chance to get to know you."

"They're a lot more willing to take that chance now that Chloe Miller has approved my presence in the community," he said drily.

"That's ridiculous. You've gotten plenty of jobs without me. What are you working on now?"

She managed to keep the conversation light and general during the meal, and she found herself relaxing. This wasn't so bad. Maybe they could just be friends. She caught herself staring at his throat, where his shirt was unbuttoned near the top and a few golden curls peeked out. It brought a vivid image of him shirtless on the ladder the first day she'd seen him, and she swallowed. *Friends don't drool over each other, Chloe. Who are you kidding?*

She tidied up her desk, tossing away the remains of the lunch as he rose. "Thank you for the sandwich."

"You're welcome." His eyes gleamed as he walked around the desk toward her. She couldn't have moved if she'd wanted to.

He took her face between his hands and set his lips

on hers, shocking her with the sudden intimacy. She lifted her own hands to circle his wrists and push him away, but somewhere in her brain, his kiss short-circuited the command, and "Push" turned into "Hang on for dear life." His mouth was warm and firm, his tongue searching for hers, curling around it with familiar intent, and her body clamored for his touch.

Against her mouth, he growled, "Have dinner with me."

"I—"

"Yes." He had lifted one hand so that his mouth could nibble its way along her jaw to her ear, where his tongue flicked lightly at a spot near her earlobe. She sucked in a startled breath, aroused beyond belief by that small touch, and he prompted again, "Yes."

"Yes." She whispered the word.

"Good." He stepped back and linked his fingers with hers, leaving her standing dazed, aching. "I'll pick you up at six."

"Not at your house," she managed to say, recalling something about principles.

"No, I'll pick you up at your house." He grinned again, deliberately misinterpreting her words. "Relax, there'll be other people around."

He pressed a short, stinging kiss on her lips, then turned for the door. "See you tonight."

"See you tonight," she whispered as the door closed behind him. She put one shaking hand to her lips, still tingling from his kisses. Oh, my.

"Chloe!"

She jumped, turning to see her father standing in his office door. He was watching Thad's retreating back through the big window. Then he turned his gaze on her. "What is the meaning of this?"

The familiar words were probably intended to cow her into a confession, just as they had on the few occasions he'd had to use them when she was small, but they had the opposite effect. She straightened, dropping her hand from her lips. "Thad brought sandwiches and we shared lunch." She began rearranging items on her desk.

"It looks like you shared more than lunch."

"Daddy! That was uncalled for. I'm an adult and I will eat with whomever I like." She enunciated the words slowly and clearly. "And do anything else I choose."

Her father's face reddened. "The Bible tells us—"

"I know what the Bible tells us, Daddy."

"Did you know I had Jean Lawman's funeral service?" The sudden change of topic was unnerving but she refused to show it.

"Her last name was Shippen."

"Her family rued the day she set eyes on him."

"Maybe they never tried to get to know him," she said. "Did *you* know Jean never told Thad she was diabetic? Do you know how they treat him when they see him?"

Her father held up both hands. "Okay, okay. Maybe I've been as guilty as everyone else of judging him too harshly." He paused, then muttered, "I still don't trust his intentions."

She was smiling, relieved that the stand-off had been resolved without words they each might have regretted. "How about mine? You've instilled morals and values in me, and I hope you'll trust me to exercise them."

Her father opened his mouth again, flapped it once like a fish on land and closed it abruptly. "You certainly are your mother's daughter sometimes." A small smile escaped the stern face he'd arranged. "She knew how to knock me down to size when I got pompous, too."

Chloe returned the smile, grateful that he was trying not to be dictatorial. "You're not pompous. Well, not much."

Thad picked her up at six as he promised, but this time her father was home. He must have been standing there waiting for the doorbell to ring because he answered the door before she could get to it. She came rushing from the kitchen where she'd been putting on lipstick in the mirror beside the pantry door, slowing her pace to a sedate walk when she realized there was no bloodshed. Yet.

"Good evening, Thaddeus," her father intoned.

"Good evening, Reverend."

She was grateful that Thad hadn't called him "Rev," as he was fond of doing. She suspected he only used the abbreviation because he knew it irritated the minister.

"Hello. I'm ready," she announced unnecessarily. As she sailed past her father, she kissed him on the cheek. "Bye, Daddy. If you're asleep when I get home, I'll see you in the morning." *Wrong thing to say.* Now her father would think she planned on staying out half the night.

But he didn't react. And to her surprise, Thad spoke again. "We won't be late. Chloe and I both have to work tomorrow."

As they walked away toward his truck, she said, "Thank you for making an effort with my father."

"No problem." He took her hand to help her into the truck.

She wanted to ask him where they were going as the

truck drove through town and out again. But as they turned onto a familiar country road, her dismay grew. He had told her they wouldn't be alone, and now he was taking her back to his house! Well, he'd just have to take her right home again, because there was no way she was going to put herself in temptation's way.

"You missed your driveway," she pointed out in a clipped tone.

"We aren't going to my house."

"Oh."

He was silent for a moment. Then he reached across the seat and took her hand, twining his fingers through hers. "I promised you we weren't going to my house. Did you think I would lie to you?"

She felt as small as a bug, and just about as squashable. "I'm sorry, Thad." Tears hovered on the edge of her voice, and he squeezed her hand gently.

"It's okay. I haven't exactly been trustworthy around you." He took his eyes off the wheel for a moment and shot her a crooked grin. "Every time I decide I'm going to keep my hands off you, I lie to *myself*."

That wasn't a statement she was going to address. To relieve the loaded silence that grew with each passing second, she asked him, "So where are we going?"

"My mother's."

His mother's. He was taking her to meet his *mother?* She pondered that for a moment, then decided it was too much effort to try to read anything into it. "Is she up to making dinner for us?"

"Sort of." He released her hand to turn into the driveway in front of a nicely kept rancher-style home on a large lot back from the road. "I got a casserole ready and set the table this morning so she wouldn't have much to do. It lets her have the illusion that she's still able to get around fairly normally." As he shut off the engine, he turned to her. "Don't let on that I told you."

"I would never do that," she said with great dignity.

He laughed as he opened her door and they started up the walk. "I know, I just wanted to loosen you up."

She punched him lightly in the shoulder—just to have an excuse to touch him, if she was truthful with herself—but before she could withdraw her hand he snagged it in midair and dragged her against his chest. "One to keep me going," he said, lowering his head.

He kissed her thoroughly, until she pushed his head away and gasped for air. "Stop! Your mother's going to see us."

His chuckle was wry and resigned. "Like my mother would care about two people kissing on her doorstep?" He reached past her and inserted a key into the front door, then swung it wide and swept her a bow. "*Entrez,* my lady."

They stepped into a living room quietly decorated in creams and moss shades. She didn't know what she was expecting, but this wasn't it. He left her there, telling her to make herself at home while he brought his mother out. Through an archway she could see a neat dining room in the same colors, the table set for three. Hmm...no risqué pictures, no red velvet. She was almost disappointed.

Then Thad appeared, supporting a frail woman in an eye-assaulting purple caftan, flowing and floor length. She stretched out a hand to Chloe as he seated her on the couch. "Hello, dear."

Thad waved at Chloe, saying "This is my mom," and disappeared into the kitchen. "Dinner'll be ready in a few minutes."

"Chloe. Such a beautiful name," the woman said. Two bright spots of rouge that matched her lipstick contrasted sharply with the pallor of her skin.

"Thank you." She smiled uncomfortably. She didn't even know what to call her! The older woman's white hair was confined in a bun, but a few strands had escaped and fell in gentle curls about her head. Searching the deep brown eyes, Chloe could see little resemblance to Thad, but his mother obviously had been a beauty in her youth.

"I'm Margreta, and I imagine you've heard my life story from every busybody in town. Believe about half of it, and you might come close." She laughed, a warm sound that made Chloe relax. "I've met your father. We had a delightful chat the first time he came. Last week, I'm afraid I was feeling a bit under the weather so he only stayed a few minutes."

That was news to Chloe. Her father had said nothing about a second visit to Thad's mother. "He enjoys the ministry," she said. "I'm sure he'll check back again and stay longer when you feel up to a visit."

"I hope so. Now—tell me about yourself. I'm going to be really nosy. Thad's never brought a girlfriend home before." Her faded eyes clouded. "Except, of course, for poor dear Jeannie."

"He's told me about Jean."

Margreta raised her eyebrows. "He hasn't been able to talk about her, even to me, since she died." She paused. "Now I *really* want to hear about *you*."

Margreta was amazingly easy to talk to. Chloe found herself explaining her dreams for the preschool, even the frustrating situation with her job. Thad called them in to dinner and they talked...about the explosion, the church's rebuilding efforts, Margreta's illness and her desire to wait as long as possible before needing around-the-clock home care. Chloe couldn't believe how matter-of-fact, how frank and realistic she was about her diagnosis.

"Don't mistake me—I'm not giving up. But I know what the odds are, and I refuse to spend my last days bald and vomiting," Margreta told her. "I can think of things I'd rather do than die, like hold my first grandchild—not that that's likely to happen anytime soon." She smiled across the table at Thad, and Chloe was tickled to see a dull red creeping up his neck.

"Time to change the subject," he announced.

"Why don't you let me clean up the kitchen while you help your mother get settled for the night?" Chloe suggested, seeing Margreta grimacing in discomfort.

"Thanks," he said. "I would appreciate that."

So Chloe washed the dishes and tidied up the remains of the meal while Thad helped his mother. After seeing her settled, Thad checked the house one more time, and they said good-night.

Six

"Your mother is wonderful," Chloe said as they settled themselves for the drive back to town.

Thad smiled. "She's something, isn't she?" Reaching across the seat, he took Chloe's hand and tugged. "You're too far away. Use the middle seat belt." When she did, he promptly laid her hand on his thigh, holding it in place with his own.

Under her palm, his thigh felt wonderfully warm. His flesh, covered by blue denim, was firm, and she resisted the urge to dig in her fingers, to test the muscle she could feel flexing each time his foot moved on the pedals. They didn't speak again until he pulled the truck to a halt in front of her house and turned off the engine.

"I had a lovely time tonight," she told him. "Your mother is delightful."

He released his seat belt and then hers, turning to face her in the seat. "I think she used the same word to describe you.'' His hand came up, sliding through the loose, silky hair around her face to the back of her neck. ''You bewitched us both.''

The night was dark and moonless, the inside of the truck a warm cocoon of intimacy. She could hear their breathing, could hear the blood as it pulsed through her veins, faster now that he was touching her again. When he exerted a slight pressure on her neck, she moved toward him willingly, her resolve of the morning forgotten under the magic his touch created.

He wrapped her in his arms as closely as possible, given their seated positions. ''What am I going to do with you?'' he murmured, almost to himself.

Her head was tilted back over his arm, her face lifted to his. She could barely make out his features, but she knew he was smiling. He was a lure and she was the helpless fish, reeled in, played out and reeled in even closer the second time. Hesitantly she lifted herself the scant distance that separated them and pressed a quick, chaste kiss to his lips.

He went still, completely motionless. His body felt like heated marble beneath her hands. Then he exhaled, a deep release of air, and his head dropped to nuzzle along her jaw until his lips met hers.

She was ready this time. She knew his taste, the way his tongue sought hers and played, the way his hands roved her body, seeking out the sweet curve of breast and hip. His fingers moved between them, and she realized that he had unbuttoned her blouse. His hand was hot against her bare skin as he dipped into the cup of her bra, freeing a breast for his attentions while his mouth left hers and moved down her throat. She barely noticed. His palm covering her breast slowly rotated in small circles, stimulating the sensitive peak until she felt an irresistible urge to shift her hips, as if that action would somehow provide relief from the heat building within her.

Then his mouth took her nipple, suckling strongly at her, and she cried out, a high, thin sound that she barely recognized as her own voice. She realized she was saying, "Please, please," pleading with him, but she didn't know what she wanted him to do.

His mouth kept up the pleasure at her breast while his other hand stroked lower, over her belly and down, bit by bit, until one bold foray traced the center seam of her slacks below her zipper. The resulting sensation almost made her jump out of her skin, and her hips lifted involuntarily against his hand. Thad groaned. He grasped her torso and lifted her, turning her so she was astride him. Between her legs she felt the hard length of him, and his hips lifted this time, pressing against her in a clear message.

"Wait." Her voice was a ragged gasp of air, but it had the effect of an enraged father with a shotgun.

Thad stopped, lifting his hands from her body as if she burned him. "Do you realize you damn near lost your innocence in the front seat of this truck?" His voice sounded as if his teeth were clenched. He also sounded furious.

"I—what?" She surfaced slowly from the storm of sexual enticement. "Yes."

"Yes *what?*" He placed his hands at her hips. "Yes, finish it, or yes, you realize what nearly happened?"

"Wait, I…can't think…" She didn't complete the thought as he lifted her ungently and dumped her on the seat beside him.

"I need a bucket of ice cubes," he announced to the roof of the truck.

She had a nearly irresistible urge to giggle, but the tone of his voice warned her that wouldn't be wise.

He opened his door and slid out, then reached in and seized her wrist, dragging her across the seat and out the door after him. "Listen to me," he said, backing her up against the side of the truck, his face in hers. "I am *not* going to have you shouting to the world that I took advantage of you, but you're making me crazy. Either we finish this or we stop seeing each other."

His words were a shock rapidly cooling the lava racing through her veins. She said, "I wouldn't accuse you of—never mind." She focused on the one thing he'd said that made sense. "You're right. We have to stop seeing each other." She put up a hand and touched the side of his face, ignoring the suppressed anger that radiated from him. "I like to think I would have stopped you, but I'm just not sure. Thad, I want to come to my marriage bed without any secrets in my past. You're the toughest test I'll ever have to pass, I guess, and I'm not all that sure of my willpower. I can't see you anymore."

He didn't speak, just turned his head, and she felt him press a kiss into her palm. "This is crazy." In contrast to the gentle touch of his mouth, his voice was harsh. "And I'm crazy for letting you get under my skin. You'd better go." He stepped away and turned his back to her.

She hesitated.

"*Go,*" he said fiercely, and she did, tears already beginning to fall as she fumbled with the front door. Behind her, she heard the quiet growl of the truck pulling away, and she felt her heart rip out of her chest and go with it. Closing the front door, she sank to her knees against the wood, both hands over her mouth to stifle the sobs she couldn't control.

She cried until her eyes stung and her nose ran, and then she cried some more. When she finally regained enough control to drag herself to her feet, she leaned against the door and took deep breaths, trying to still the involuntary sobs that continued to choke her. Thank goodness her father's room was at the back of the house, she thought. *He'd die of shock if he came down here and found me like this.*

A knock on the other side of the door had her whirling away from it as if the wood had come alive. Her heart leaped and she yanked the door open, not even considering that it might be a stranger. She hurled herself at Thad, closing the door behind her, and felt herself become whole, healed as his arms closed around her. Unable to control herself, she began to sob again.

"Sh-h-h." He rocked her as if she were a child, using his shirt to blot her tears. "I'm sorry, I shouldn't have left that way." He sought her mouth, and she met him halfway, sharing gentle kisses of comfort, dragging her mouth over his skin as he kissed her temples, her forehead, her nose and returned to her mouth again. But he lifted his head when comfort began to turn to passion again.

"I can't take any more of this." He was panting heavily, his chest heaving up and down like a racehorse that had just won the Kentucky Derby.

"I'm sorry," she whispered, her voice hitching. Then, a moment later, "Why am *I* apologizing? You're the one who left and came back!"

"Didn't you want me to?"

"You know I did." She wrapped her arms around him, feeling the ridges of muscle along his spine beneath her palms, feeling him pressed against every part of her from head to toe and wanting him more than she wanted to take her next breath. "But nothing's changed. I wish I could be the kind of woman you need. But I can't. I'm old-fashioned, I guess."

"Then we'll get married."

"That's not what I meant!" Shock waves battered at her mind.

Rearing back, she put some space between them. She knew he'd uttered the words in jest, but the mere thought made her heart race with alarming speed, and she squelched the longing, afraid it would show in her eyes.

"I meant it, though." He grinned, his crooked smile that she knew meant he was laughing at himself. "I never pictured myself doing this, but—" Seizing her hand, he dropped to one knee before her. "Chloe Miller, will you marry me?"

Mortified, she tugged at him, trying to get him on his feet again. "Thad, you don't really want—"

He shut her up simply by pulling her onto his knee and placing a large hand over her mouth. "Yes, *I really want*. And what's more, I really want to marry you. I need you. If this is the only way I can have you, I'll take it. I can think of plenty of things worse than being married to you for the rest of our lives."

As proposals went, his stank. So did his reasoning. And his timing. A girl with swollen eyes and a runny nose was in no shape to consider a proposal of marriage. She should be insulted, but she had to restrain herself from shouting, "Yes!" and waking her father to perform the ceremony right there and then. Still, a small voice inside her cautioned her. *He doesn't love you. He was married before to someone he didn't love.*

But he wants me. He said he needs me.

Do you want to marry someone who doesn't love you on the off chance that one day he will?

Yes!

Rising from his knee, she said, "I'll consider it. But I won't rush into anything."

"I can live with that." He rose and drew her into his arms again, tucking her head under his chin. Their bodies were sandwiched together, and she could tell he was aroused, but for the moment this embrace was one of sweetness and comfort. He stroked a hand down over her hair. "Don't make it too complicated in your head."

"I'm afraid it won't work," she whispered.

"Why wouldn't it work? I'm a good provider. We're going to be great together in bed. I'd be faithful to you, and I'd love our children."

Children. He knew how to get to her, all right. Images of small, wriggling towheads with dimples danced across her mental screen. She banished them. "Why me?"

He was silent for a moment and her heart sank. She'd made him see reason. He really didn't want to marry her.

"You're the only person who's ever looked past what they heard about me. Even Jean, I think, went out with me at first to spite her straitlaced parents. You believe in me," he said simply. Then he chuckled, and she felt it through every cell in her body. "Besides, I'm afraid I'll die of terminal sperm suppression if you won't marry me."

She was glad it was dark on the porch because she was blushing again. "I still need time. Time away from you to think. You could get me to agree to just about anything if you really tried." Those words skated dangerously close to a declaration of love, and she rushed to cover them. "I won't make you wait too long for an answer."

"Twenty-four hours is too long for me," he grumbled. But she could tell he wasn't unhappy. "Right now you are going inside to get some sleep." He brushed a last kiss across her lips, lingering for a moment before pulling himself away. "This is what started all the trouble in the first place. I'll see you tomorrow."

Six days later she awoke with a feeling of anticipation. As she stretched, she remembered why. It was Sunday. Thad had agreed to go to church with her today. In fact, it had been his idea.

"If I'm marrying a preacher's daughter, I'd better get used to going to church."

"You can come to church with me, but I haven't agreed to marry you," she reminded him.

To which he had smugly replied, "Yet."

Lordy, what was she going to do? All she could think about was him. And more accurately, his body. She'd never realized how sexual excitement could cloud a person's judgment. For the first time she could understand how people could get so carried away by passion that they forgot principles, morals...their names...

How was she supposed to make a momentous decision about her future, when all she wanted was to feel him against her again. All she had to do was see him, and her breath grew shorter, her nerve endings began to twitch, and her body grew...restless. She'd told Thad she needed to be away from him so she could consider his proposal, but she hadn't realized he'd have to be on the other side of the planet before she could think rationally. She was no closer today to giving him an answer than she had been on Monday night.

Marrying a man who didn't love her was a stupid thing to do. She knew she'd be courting heartbreak. On the other hand, heartbreak would be a surety if she told him no. So why not take a chance?

Her father didn't like him. Thad didn't like her father. They were like two dogs vying for dominance when they were in the same room, circling, sniffing, calculating weaknesses and plotting attack strategies. Her father loved her, had cared for her all her life. But she wasn't considering marrying her father. If she married Thad, would she have to choose between them?

She jumped out of bed and briskly threw the covers to the foot of the bed to air out while she showered. She was making herself insane, going around and around with these questions. If only she had a crystal ball. Or hindsight. That would be a help.

Thad met her in the vestibule right before the service. She hadn't told her father he was coming, mostly because she didn't want to argue with him, and she saw his eyes widen momentarily in the middle of a conversation with one of the ushers.

Quickly, before he could approach, she took Thad's arm. "Here's a bulletin. Let's find a seat."

There was a slight ripple of interest, a wave of sudden whispering and rustling as they walked up the aisle and slid into a pew. She hoped Thad didn't realize it was unusual.

A whisper came from somewhere behind them. "...I can't believe she is dating him. Are you sure?"

"Shh." Another speaker.

And then, "You know who his mother is, don't you?"

"I know. Shh."

"Wonder when she'll start to show? There has to be a good reason he's here with her."

"*Would you shut up? They'll hear you.*"

She could hardly breathe. A rage rose up inside her, deeper and stronger than she'd ever known anger could get. Her hands were shaking. How dare they? *How dare they?* They should be ashamed to step inside a church. She'd never been tempted, ever, to create a scene, but she had to exert every ounce of self-control she had not to turn around and blast the old biddie.

She glanced at Thad out of the corner of her eye. A muscle jumped in his cheek but that was the only sign that he'd heard. Impulsively she reached over and laid one hand atop his where it rested in his lap. For a minute she thought he was going to ignore her, and then he turned his palm up and squeezed her hand.

She ached for him. How horrible to have known this all your life, to have people *expect* you to sleep with every girl who's seen with you. After they were married, she was going to use birth control for a while, just to prove—

After they were married. Saying it, even in her head, gave her a little thrill. Why deny it, deny him, any longer? She loved him and wanted to marry him, he wanted her, and they would make it work from there.

For the rest of the service, she held on to his hand, not even letting go when they rose for the hymns and prayers. She hoped those old crones were getting an eyeful.

Her father delivered the benediction, and the organist broke into the postlude as people began to chat again.

She stood, and Thad rose with her. Around them, people were shuffling out of their pews and herding down the aisles to the exits. What better place than here? Thad had turned away from her, preparing to leave the pew so she could precede him up the aisle, but she put a hand on his arm.

He looked back, his raised brows inquiring.

"Yes."

He looked blank. "What?"

She couldn't prevent a brilliant smile from spreading across her face, so happy did she feel all of a sudden. "Yes, I'll marry you."

His eyes narrowed and beneath her hand, the muscled forearm tensed. His chest swelled visibly before he exhaled heavily. "You picked a hell of a time to tell me," he muttered beneath his breath. "Do you know what I'd like to do with you right now?"

Her breath came faster as she registered the sexual intent in his rough voice, and she whispered, "Yes."

He lifted a hand and caressed her cheek. "But I don't want to give these folks any more shocks today. Just hold those thoughts until I get you alone."

They told her father that evening after dinner.

"Daddy, I hope you'll be happy for me," she concluded, talking on and on to cover the stunned silence that followed her announcement. Thad had come in after dinner as they'd arranged, and they faced him together in the sitting room.

"Do you really know what you're doing?" Reverend Miller demanded. "You two barely know each other."

"We know each other in the ways that count," she responded steadily.

"This is for the rest of your lives. It can't be undone if things crop up that change the way you feel."

Thad cleared his throat. "We don't intend to undo it,

ever. I'll take good care of her." He hesitated. "I know I'm not what you would have chosen for Chloe, but—"

"But I'm happy with the choice I've made," she finished. "And I hope you'll give us your blessing."

The minister sank into a chair. He suddenly looked every one of his sixty-one years. He held out his hand to Chloe. "Of course I'll give you my blessing."

They drove out to tell Margreta their news afterward. She was as thrilled as Thad predicted she would be, and her bubbling enthusiasm was a joy after her father's reserved reception. They didn't stay long, though, since they both had to work the next morning.

Back in the truck he said, "What do you want to do about living arrangements? I draw the line at moving in with you and your father."

She giggled. "And here I was cleaning out the spare bedroom for you."

He put his hand on her thigh and the warm clasp made her shiver. "You don't stand a chance of sleeping in a bed without me, once that ring is on your finger, protective papa or not."

They were passing his trailer, and he suddenly swung the truck into the driveway. "I guess we can live here for a couple of months while we look for a house."

"A house to buy?"

He kissed the tip of her nose and reached for the door handle. "Come on. You can take a quick look through my cupboards so you can start thinking about what you'd like to add or get rid of."

He left her in the tiny kitchen, telling her he wanted to check something in the office. She felt strange, opening cabinets and examining the details of his life, almost like she was snooping, and she had to remind herself that one day they would be sharing everything. They still hadn't discussed a wedding date, but Thad wouldn't want to wait too long, she was sure. Neither had they talked much yet about what kind of wedding they wanted. The only thing she knew for sure was that she wanted it small, intimate and memorable. Once she'd dreamed of walking down the aisle of the old church with six bridesmaids waiting for her, the pews full of every face she knew, but she couldn't imagine putting Thad through an ordeal like that, and frankly, it sounded a lot less appealing when she was faced with the thought of organizing it all.

Quickly she made a mental inventory of the little living room. She had some furniture that her father would insist she take with her, but that might have to wait until they found a house. A house—she could hardly wait!

Two hands came down on her shoulders and she shrieked before she could control herself.

"Daydreaming?" Thad turned her around and surveyed her shining eyes.

"I'm so happy!" She flung her arms around his neck and dragged his head down for a kiss.

He staggered back a step under her exuberance, but lifted his arms to loosely circle her waist. "Remind me to make you happy often."

Laughing, she stroked her palms over his broad shoulders, down his arms and back up, her love for him welling up from the place in her heart where she kept it hidden. What a sweet luxury to be able to touch him any way she liked! Her eyes were level with his throat, where she could see golden curls peeping from the neck of his sport shirt. Acting on impulse, she leaned forward and kissed him right there, in the hollow of his throat. He didn't move and, feeling greatly daring, she kissed the spot again, this time lingering over the kiss so that her tongue slipped over the salty roughness of his flesh.

Beneath her mouth, a groan vibrated. "Woman, you're testing my self-restraint. If you want to be a virgin on your wedding day, you'd better stop that."

"Oh, come on, Thad." She was in too good a mood to be deterred. "Let's just neck a little."

"Neck a little?" he echoed. "That's like telling a bee just to sting a little." But he lifted her and sat down on the couch, holding her cradled in one arm.

She slid her arms up around his neck and tilted her head back. "I can't wait until we can do this every night."

His mouth met hers as he muttered, "Neither can I." He tasted her thoroughly, teasing her with his tongue as his free hand stroked up and down her back, circling forward until he was exploring the tip of her breast through her cotton blouse. Surrendering herself to sensation, she closed her eyes as he unbuttoned the garment, arching up as he unclasped her bra, then gasping when he took her in his mouth. For long moments he feasted on her breasts. Her toes curled, and in her abdomen a taut wanting urged her to assuage it. His lips were still at her breast when his hand slipped down, stroking her belly and dipping one long finger beneath the waistband of her jeans.

She moaned, knowing only that she liked the caress. Immediately his mouth returned to cover hers for another of those deep, drugging kisses. He traced small circles over her belly and she realized he'd unbuttoned her pants, but she didn't care. Her fingers speared through his hair to cradle his skull. The circles swept a fraction lower with each pass, brushing the nest of curls at the joining of her legs. She trembled in his arms, moaning again beneath his mouth.

He lifted his head, and his eyes glittered as he looked down over her body. A wash of color stained his cheekbones, and then her eyes closed as he arched her back over his arm and his head descended to suckle her again. Between her legs, his fingers were sliding lower and lower, rubbing repeatedly over a spot that had her arching in his arms, quivering with tension. One long finger probed more intimately, and then her eyes flew open as that questing finger slid up inside her, pressing and retreating repeatedly. A smile was on his lips. "Relax," he whispered. "Let it happen." The sound of his hoarse voice was a trigger for her body's response. All at once great waves of rhythmic muscle spasms swept her, thrusting her body against his hand over and over again. She cried out and turned her face into his shoulder as her body completed its sensual dance, sucking in a strangled breath as his finger slipped away from her, brushing against super-sensitized flesh.

Thad's chest was heaving beneath her cheek. "Oh, baby," he whispered. "You're going to burn me alive." Slowly she realized that his body was still tense and rigid beneath hers.

Embarrassment nearly choked her. He'd touched her in ways she'd never dreamed could be so exciting, and she'd—she'd had an orgasm in his arms without even having intercourse! She'd read about it, but had never imagined the printed words applying to *her*. "I'm sorry," she said against his shirt. "I should have waited until we were married."

Above her head Thad gave a bark of laughter. "Isn't that supposed to be my line?"

She raised her eyes to his, expecting him to be sullen

and angry that she'd—gone ahead without him, but he was smiling, his eyes intense as they swept her face. "You don't have a thing to be sorry about. Did you like that?"

She felt terribly shy, answering such an intimate question. Her eyes studied a button on his shirt, but she nodded. "I liked it."

His eyes crinkled at the corners, and she relaxed, enjoying the moment and snuggling against him.

He groaned, a loud, harsh sound of pain, and she shot bolt upright on his lap. "What's wrong? Did I hurt you?"

Thad was laughing, a rueful sound as he lifted her to one side and stood up. "No, I've just got a serious case of circuit overload."

She could hardly miss it, seated as she was at eye level. A heavy bulge strained the fabric of his jeans, a bulge that she knew meant he was…aroused.

"I'm sorry," she said again, helplessly. What was she supposed to say in a situation like this? "I really didn't mean for us to end up like this."

"It's okay." He took her hand and drew her to her feet. "But we'd better get out of here before I give in to the urge to carry you in there—" he jerked his head in the direction of the office that doubled as his bedroom "—and lay you down on that bed without a stitch of clothing and—"

"Stop!" She put a palm over his mouth, feeling the hated blush stealing up her cheeks again. "I get the picture." She buttoned her jeans self-consciously and stepped toward the door, then turned and gave him a weak smile. "Thank you. For not—for waiting."

"You can thank me after we're married."

As they drove away from the little haven, she heard

his low chuckle through the dark. "If that was necking a little, I can't wait to see what 'a lot' will be like."

He deserved an A in Self-control 101. She'd been so hot and responsive in his arms last night that he'd nearly forgotten how important it was to her to wait to consummate the marriage. *Consummate the marriage?* He was starting to sound like Chloe. He'd heard that's what happened to people who spent their lives together. The thought was oddly pleasing, and he whistled as he drove through town.

It was Tuesday afternoon, the day Chloe's father was out of the office. Thad was hoping to catch him at home and it looked like he was in luck. Parking the truck, he strode onto the front porch and boldly rang the bell. *This* wasn't going to be fun, but she was worth it. A grin spread foolishly over his face as he remembered how she'd flown apart for him last night. She was definitely worth it.

The door opened and Thad quickly wiped the smile off his face. "Good afternoon, sir." He supposed it was a bit premature to start calling him "Pop."

"Thad, is something wrong?" The minister didn't invite him in.

"No, sir. I just came to ask a favor of you."

Five minutes later Reverend Miller's face drew together in a fierce scowl. "You can't plan a wedding in a week."

"We don't need a lot of planning for a small ceremony."

"I always assumed she'd be married here, in the old church." The older man paused, a fleeting expression of sorrow passing over it. "That, of course, is no longer possible, but I'm not going to deprive my daughter of a ceremony that includes all the people who have watched her grow up.''

"Chloe doesn't want a big wedding. A small, simple ceremony will make her happiest.''

"She doesn't know what would make her happiest.''

The implication being, of course, that marrying *him* wasn't going to make her happy, either. Thad took a deep breath. The old man was getting under his skin with his constant, veiled criticisms. What the hell had happened to "forgive and forget"?

Trying another tack, he asked, "Can you honestly say that you want a big church wedding? You want to give Chloe to me in front of a hundred of your friends?''

No response. From the look on the rev's face, the thought was less than palatable. Sensing a weak spot, Thad used his last round. He'd hoped this wouldn't be necessary, but he'd be damned if this old man was going to keep Chloe away from him a day longer than he'd planned. "We need to be married as soon as possible, sir.''

"You need..." Reverend Miller's face flushed a deep tomato shade. His hands closed into fists on the desktop, and he was silent for a moment. When he raised his head, there was weary resignation in his eyes. "I see.''

Thad seriously doubted that he did see. In fact, he hoped the reverend couldn't see the carnal thoughts bouncing around in his head every time he thought about marrying the man's daughter. But since the minister didn't question him further, he let him jump to his own conclusions. It wasn't his fault, was it, if Chloe's father assumed she was pregnant? Really. He should have more faith in her. The woman's morals were set in cement.

At least, until he started kissing her.

He realized the rev was waiting for him to speak, and suddenly he had a flash of how the man must feel. "Reverend—" he hesitated "—I promise you I'll take care of your daughter. She'll be the most important thing in my life. And you'll always be welcome in our home."

The minister studied him for a moment, and Thad wondered what he was thinking. Just as he decided the olive branch might as well have been used for kindling, the pastor said, "Thank you, Thaddeus. I appreciate that." He made an effort to smile. "I suppose we'd better make this as perfect as possible. She'll never get married again."

Seven

"**W**ant to get married tomorrow?"

She smiled and glanced across the desk at Thad, who had brought a sandwich to the office again. She didn't like to leave on Fridays because her father was out until about 2:00 p.m. and there was no one else to cover. Her heart had jumped a little at his words, but she forced herself to return his teasing in kind. "That would be nice. What time?"

"The ceremony is set for four o'clock. That should give you most of the day to do all the stuff brides do." There was a ring of truth in his casual tone that got Chloe's attention.

"You *are* joking, right?"

He grinned. "Am I?"

"Of course you are." But she still wasn't certain. "Aren't you?"

He stood and came around the desk, leaning a hip

against it and taking one of her hands. "No, I'm not joking."

Butterfly wings launched a mad assault in her stomach, excitement and apprehension in equal parts. "But, Thad, we can't possibly—"

"But if we could, what would you say?"

Wide-eyed, she knew she didn't need to consider. Still, it wouldn't be good to let him know how badly she wanted to take advantage of his offer before he withdrew it. "It would be the craziest thing I've ever done."

His lips twisted in a wry smile. "Now there's a ringing endorsement."

"I didn't mean it *that* way. I—"

He leaned forward, placing a finger against her lips. "Just listen. There's a pretty little church down in Maryland reserved for four o'clock. There will be flowers and music and a minister."

She thought her heart might force its way right out of her chest, it was beating so hard. A wave of longing rushed through her. Hesitantly, searching his eyes for reaction, she whispered, "All right."

"Great." Though the word was restrained, his body seemed to lose its subtle taut-wire tension. "We can go over to the courthouse this afternoon for the license. There's no waiting period in Maryland."

"But, Thad, I can't just leave."

As if it had been prearranged, her father strolled through the door. "Chloe, I won't need you this afternoon. Take some time off. I'm sure you and Thad have things to do."

She stared at him. Her father was smiling at her. Thad had a ridiculous grin on his face. They both looked extremely pleased with themselves. It *had* been prearranged! "Are you two in cahoots?" She shook her head, slightly dazed by the thought. "I never thought I'd live long enough to see you agree on anything."

Both men had the grace to look slightly ashamed.

Thad recovered first. "So what do you think?"

She spread her hands as the butterflies changed into champagne bubbles of giddiness. "It sounds as if you two have taken care of everything." Hastily she tidied her desk and retrieved her purse. "Oh, no. We can't get married tomorrow. I haven't had the dress altered yet." Her disappointment was so keen she could feel tears at the back of her eyes.

"Oh, by the way," her father said. "Did I forget to tell you? Barbara Halteran is coming by the house in thirty minutes. She promised me she could have the dress ready for you tomorrow."

"Oh, Daddy." She embraced her father in a tearful hug. "Thank you. You don't know how much this means to me."

Reverend Miller kissed her cheek as he released her. "I only have one little girl. If you have to get married, we might as well make the best of it."

Thad cleared his throat. "Are you ready? As soon as your fitting is over we'll drive down to Maryland."

Thad stood at the altar, fidgeting while the organist played some churchy-sounding tune. The sooner this was over, the better. He wanted to get a ring on Chloe's finger before anyone talked her out of marrying him. If they waited very long, he was sure she'd have second thoughts.

The idea of living without her had become an impossibility. He hadn't looked at another woman since the day he'd met her. No other woman would ever be

Chloe, with her funny little notions of propriety in public and her astonishing habit of turning into a wild woman in private—and that was as far as he'd better take *that* line of thought, if he didn't want her father to come after him with a gun. But it was more than just the physical thing. Although "the physical thing" had a lot to recommend it. He liked the way she defended him, the gentleness with which she treated his mother, and even more, he had gotten used to the way she believed in him, totally and without question. She enhanced his life in more ways than he could count, and there was no chance he was going to let her get away.

If anyone had told him three months ago that he'd be standing at the altar, *of his own free will,* waiting for his bride, he'd have laughed himself silly. One experience with marriage had cured him forever. Until Chloe.

Just then the music changed. He looked toward the back of the church, and his breath caught in his throat as she came into view.

She had the fingers of one hand tucked through her father's arm. The other held the trailing spray of roses he'd ordered. He hadn't seen her dress before the ceremony. It had been her mother's, a delicate ivory satin that clung to her breasts and displayed her tiny waist. It had a puffy floor-length skirt and she had tucked some pretty, fragile-looking white stuff among the curls she'd pulled away from her face. She looked beautiful, and breakable.

Her face was glowing, but as he took her hand, he felt her fingers trembling. Then her father stepped up before them and began the marriage ceremony, and he felt her jolt. He gave her a reassuring smile—he hadn't told her that her father was performing the ceremony.

It went fast, faster than he'd imagined, and in the

space of a few minutes, he was a married man. As he
slipped his ring onto her finger, he thought, strangely
enough, of his mother. She couldn't make the trip, but
he'd promised to bring Chloe by later so Margreta could
see her in her gown. When he kissed his wife—*his
wife!*—he kept it light and tender, mindful of her father's eagle eye. Then it was over. They signed the marriage certificate, he paid the two witnesses—the elderly
man and woman who were caretakers of the church
property—and she clung to his arm as he led her up the
aisle to the clicking of the photographer's camera.

He'd gone to great lengths to make this day special.
The pretty little church was on the historic register—
she'd bet her father had had a hand in getting it opened
for them. And if she'd had a moment's sadness, knowing she would never say her vows in their old church,
she'd pushed it away. Her father...he'd been better,
calmer and kinder to Thad than she'd ever have believed. If he was still opposed to his new son-in-law,
he kept it to himself and did a magnificent acting job.

As she stood in the middle of the dressing room in
the luxurious bridal suite he'd booked in a nearby hotel,
slowly removing her mother's wedding dress, it hit her
fully that tonight Thad would make love to her. He'd
kept her too busy in the past twenty-four hours to think
about it.

Then her fingers stilled on the buttons of the sleeve.
She was wrong. Tonight, *she'd* be the one making love.
Thad would be having sex. She'd known that was how
it would be when she married him. She'd taken this
chance, hoping he'd love her back someday. But he
didn't love her now.

In her heart she knew the only reason he had rushed

her to the altar was because he couldn't wait any longer
for the sex. All day, she'd pretended otherwise, but deep
down, she was sure he never would have proposed at
all if she hadn't refused to sleep with him. It took some
of the joy out of her recollections of the day, but if she
was honest with herself, it didn't matter what his motives were. She would have married him in a wedding
chapel in Las Vegas if he'd asked her. Because she
loved him.

And now, according to the laws of the state of Maryland and the vows they'd exchanged before her father,
her life was bound with his. She had literally left her
family to cleave to him, as the Biblical passage in the
Book of Ruth said.

"Chloe? Do you need help getting out of that dress?"
Thad was on the other side of the door.

She felt shy and awkward about the moments to
come, but even more, she didn't want to be alone with
her thoughts any longer, so she reached out and turned
the knob.

Thad was still wearing the dark suit pants he'd worn
to the wedding and to the restaurant afterward, but he
was definitely wilting around the edges. His tie dangled
around his neck, and the first three buttons of his shirt
had come open. He was in his stocking feet, and his
jacket had disappeared.

His eyes darkened as he looked across the small
space at her. "Come here."

She came.

Under his skillful lips she forgot her reservations, her
fears. This was Thad, and she loved him. Everything
else would take care of itself.

They were both breathing hard when he lifted his
head. "Turn around," he said, his hands at her waist

urging her to spin. She felt the warmth of his fingers moving down her back, freeing her from the dress, and as the last button came open, he slipped his hands inside it, caressing her ribs and moving inexorably around to the front of her body. One hand cupped a breast and the other pressed lightly against her stomach, drawing her back against him. As he did so, he dropped his head to nuzzle along the side of her neck and press open-mouthed kisses along her shoulder.

Then he removed his hands, pausing for a moment at her back before he turned her again. Setting his fingers at the neckline of the gown, he eased it down as she slipped her arms from the long sleeves, until it was a bouffant puddle around her knees. Her bra went with it, and belatedly she realized he'd unhooked it. Almost reflexively, her arms came up to cross over her breasts in an age-old gesture of feminine modesty.

A small smile played around Thad's lips. Reaching out, he drew one of her hands to his mouth and kissed her fingers. She'd never thought of fingers as erotic zones before, but as his tongue swirled around each digit and gently flicked at the deep valleys between, she forgot all about her modesty as her body responded to the warm, liquid caress. Then he took her other hand, holding both her arms at her sides, exposing her body fully to his view.

Without a word, he looked at her, and she could actually feel the heat in the path his eyes traced over her. When his eyes returned to hers, they had gone a dark, stormy blue that promised satisfaction and demanded surrender.

All she wore now was a minuscule pair of panties. Silken hose were held in place by ruffled garters. She'd never felt so naked in her life.

Slowly he raised her hands, placing the palms against his lightly furred chest. Lifting his own hands, he placed them on the slender curves below her waist. "Beautiful," he said hoarsely. "You're beautiful." His eyes narrowed as he stroked a large palm over each of her breasts, slowly circling and rolling until she felt her nipples rising into taut buds beneath his fingers and her entire body vibrate with tension. A wanton throbbing spread low in her abdomen, and she closed her eyes, raising her own hands to clasp the heavy musculature of his shoulders. Just when she thought she would die if he didn't do *something,* his hands slid slowly down, over her hips and around to her bottom, curving under the tiny panties, and she gasped as he caressed the deep groove between her buttocks.

Then he sank to his knees before her. She looked down at his bright hair, trembling with new sensations. Taking his hands from her bottom, he carefully slipped her hose and garters off, one at a time, brushing the insides of her thighs as he did so and causing her to suck in a sharp breath. His eyes were intent as he hooked his thumbs in the panties and drew them down, as well.

She was nude before him, acutely aware of him kneeling before her. Lifting his arm, he circled her hips and tugged her gently forward, laying his head against her belly for a moment before turning to her and kissing her navel and lower body just above her nest of curls. She felt so strange, as if her legs wouldn't support her any longer, and as if he sensed it he rose.

He lifted her free of the dress at her feet and into his arms, carrying her to the big bed in the bridal bedroom and placing her atop the sheets. Leaving her for a moment, he quickly stripped off his shirt and tie, pants and socks. She had turned her head to watch, and she was both embarrassed and fascinated by the sight of him clad only in low-slung briefs that did nothing to hide his reaction to her. Her embarrassment faded as the passion he aroused in her blossomed, and her body recalled the peak to which he'd taken her once before.

"Hurry," she whispered through suddenly dry lips, in someone else's voice, and he laughed, the sound little more than a growl deep in his throat as he removed his briefs.

"Tonight we're taking our time," he said, placing a knee on the mattress and moving to lie on his side next to her. Against her hip, his hot silky strength throbbed. He laid a large hand on her belly as he leaned over her, his mouth taking hers in a deep imitation of possession that lasted until she thought she might die if he didn't move faster. She wound her arms around his neck, trying to pull him closer, and he allowed it. His chest felt as if it held a furnace inside where it pressed against her sensitive breasts. She twisted her torso, rubbing herself against him, and his voice was strained as he said, "Little wildcat. You make me so crazy I forget you're new to this."

She smiled against his lips, then gasped as the hand on her belly moved slowly but inexorably down, down, over her woman's mound and between her legs, cupping her heat in his palm. Unused to such intimacy, she panicked for a moment, and the sensual woman who'd replaced her vanished beneath inhibition. Instinctively, she tried to close her legs but the motion only trapped his hand more effectively. He kissed her again, using his teeth and tongue until she relaxed and forgot the hand lying between her thighs.

Then she remembered abruptly, as his stealthy fingers

began a steady, circling stroke, growing bolder with each caress. Heat flared low in her belly. As if of their own will, her thighs relaxed enough to allow him better access, and her hips began to move against his hand. Then a long finger probed her, and she arched against his hand in startlement, not able to tell whether she wanted him to stop or wanted more. It didn't hurt, it just felt so... "Ah. Are you ready for me?" Before she realized what was happening, he eased his weight onto her, lying fully atop her, covering her from head to foot with his big body.

His big, *aroused* body. She could feel the hard length of him prodding gently at the V of her legs, and excitement spiraled within her so fiercely that her hands shook where they clung to his broad back. He reached down between them and suddenly, shockingly, he was *there,* poised at the portal of her body.

His eyes blazed down at her as he slowly pushed forward, and she whimpered at the inexorable pressure. He bared his teeth and dropped his head, nipping her neck less than gently, and she arched in surprise.

As she did, he thrust his hips forward. For one long moment the pressure increased to an unbearable level, and then her body yielded and he slid past the barrier to lodge within her.

She squeaked in surprise and sudden pain, her body freezing in protest and he smiled grimly down at her. "It gets better, baby. I promise. The first time is always rough."

He held perfectly still within her. As her body adjusted to the full sensation, accepting him more easily, she could feel his heartbeat against her and within her, hear the air rushing in and out of his lungs, rub her fingers along the slick, sweated flesh of his back and feel the muscled power. As she began to relax, she realized that it wasn't terribly painful, and her confidence began to return. Her hands dipped lower, palming tight, muscled buttocks, and he groaned. "That's not such a good idea right now."

"Oh?" She tried to smile flirtatiously, but her lips trembled.

"Ah, honey." He levered his hips a fraction away from her and then flexed again, pushing back into her. "I have to... I can't wait."

She started to tell him it was all right, that it only hurt a little bit, but his body began to move against her again, more urgently and more powerfully than anything she'd been expecting, and suddenly it hurt a lot. He was too big, moving too fast. She squirmed beneath him, trying to push him away as tears sprang to her eyes. Why had it felt so good before?

Against her sensitive flesh, his body moved faster and faster, sliding in and out of her in measured strokes as his breath whistled in and out. Then, just when she thought she couldn't bear being split asunder like this for another second, he arched against her, embedding himself as deeply as he could fit, and she felt the small pulses of his release against her inner walls, an intimacy greater even than what had just occurred. A few more times, less and less violently, he arched again, until he was lying limp over her, his dead weight pressing her into the mattress.

And even in the discomfort she felt, she still was moved to raise her hands and cradle his skull, to run her fingers over his blond hair, feeling somehow as if *he* were the one who needed comforting.

Finally, he stirred. "I'm sorry."

She wanted to tell him it was all right, but she

couldn't. It *wasn't* all right. *She* wasn't all right. She settled for "I know."

Still nestled snug within her, he raised himself on his elbows and said through his teeth, "No, you don't. You don't know one damn thing." He lifted himself away then, sliding off the bed and padding naked into the bathroom.

She lay watching as he walked away, confusion and unhappiness a sudden tight ball in her chest as she took in his tight, round buttocks and the ropes of muscle that rippled across his back, the long, firm legs and the way his shoulders tapered to his trim waist. His occupation certainly kept him fit. A wave of weariness washed over her, and she yawned. It had been an eventful, draining day. Reaching down to the foot of the bed, she had just pulled the sheet over her when Thad returned, carrying a washcloth in his hand.

She watched without comprehension until he flipped the edge of the sheet back, baring her body. Automatically she started to cover herself with her hands.

"Don't." The single word stopped her hands in mid-air.

She knew he was right. It was silly to be shy in front of him now that they were married, particularly given what had just occurred between them. But that didn't stop the hated feeling of heat, the blush, from rising to her cheeks.

Thad's face softened, and he reached out, tracing the curve of her cheek with a gentle finger. "I can't believe you're blushing *now*."

Her face grew even redder as his gaze swept down over her exposed body. "I know. It's a little late for modesty."

Then she gasped as he gently parted her thighs and

cleaned *there* with the washcloth. He was careful, and it didn't hurt, but she turned her face away. It might be silly, but it was going to take some time before she got used to his casual attitude about nude bodies.

"How do you feel?" He tossed the washcloth in the general direction of the bathroom.

"Fine." She moved experimentally. It wasn't a lie, she did feel fine, although she wasn't about to explore to see where she might hurt. At least her body felt fine, she amended. Her mind was still whirling with disappointment despite her exhaustion.

He crawled back into bed and reached for her, pulling the sheets up over them both and settling her in the curve of his arm, one hand resting low on her belly. "It'll be better next time."

She hoped so. She really hoped so. But she wasn't holding her breath.

His arms were warm around her, and despite the soreness in her body, she enjoyed being cuddled and coddled. She was almost asleep, still in his embrace, drifting away into slumber, when a disturbing thought burst into her mind.

"We didn't use any birth control tonight."

Instantly she felt the tension in his body, in the way the arm beneath her stiffened, and she sensed he was wide awake—he must not have thought about it, either, until she said something.

"Is that a problem?" His voice was in her ear, sounding strangely cool and remote, not like his usual lazy, teasing self at all.

"Well, isn't it?" She was suddenly uncertain. "We need time to get used to living together."

"We have the rest of our lives for that." He paused,

and his tone was softer when he went on. "I wouldn't mind if you got pregnant tonight."

She considered his words for a while. "I think I'll mind. I'm barely used to being a bride, let alone a mother."

The hand on her belly flexed, then relaxed. "We can worry about it if it happens."

"And from now on, for a little while, at least, we'll use birth control. I'll go to the doctor—"

"No." His voice was as hard as she'd ever heard it. "I'll take care of it for a while. We can talk about it again in a few months and decide." Levering himself over her on his palms, he dropped his head and kissed her, and even knowing what she might provoke if she aroused him, she couldn't keep herself from responding. As he lay back, he urged her onto her side so that her back was to him, pressing her against his chest, his thighs cradling hers. How strange. She shouldn't feel so comfortable. She'd never slept with another person in her whole life. And yet—this felt *right*. She felt safe and protected, and as another wave of weariness swept over her, she forgot her concerns and closed her eyes.

He opened his eyes slowly, immediately aware of the sweet warmth of feminine flesh at his side. Chloe. His wife. He was on his stomach, head buried in the pillow, and carefully he raised himself to his elbows so he could look down at her.

She slept on her side, facing him, her hands curled up beneath her chin in loose fists. One leg was stretched straight, the other drawn over it with the knee bent. Her skin looked soft and rosy, her lips smiling the faintest bit even in repose. The sheet had slipped down across the curve of her hip, leaving her upper body bared to his view. One breast was hidden by her arms but the other peeked out from beneath them, the pink nipple capping it soft.

He could watch her all day. And he did, for a long time, as the room grew lighter with the approach of dawn.

It seemed like a miracle. Every morning he could wake like this and find her sleeping by his side. The only flaw, he thought, thinking critically of what he was taking her home to, was the trailer. She deserved better, and as soon as she could find a house she liked, he'd buy it and move her into it. One more little tie to bind her to him.

He honestly hadn't thought about birth control last night, because it didn't matter to him. Well, that wasn't strictly true. As far as he was concerned, the sooner she was pregnant, the better. He'd been unprepared for the surge of longing that shot through him when she mentioned having a child. Maybe then he'd stop thinking that she was going to look at him—*really* look at him— one day and wake up to realize she didn't want to spend her life with him.

But it was more than that. He wanted kids. He wanted to come home to shrieking, giggling chaos, to sticky fingers and stuffed animals. He wanted to watch his child grow and change, to look for Chloe's features, or his own, in a tiny face, to celebrate milestones like first words and first grade.

Until she was really and truly pregnant, until he could put his hands over her belly and feel his child moving within her, he would harbor a small knot of fear deep inside. Maybe she really didn't want his child and was just putting off the decision—

"Deep thoughts this morning?" A warm hand reached out and stroked his cheek.

Without thinking, he turned his head and kissed her fingers, then lost his balance and fell atop her as she put both arms around his neck and yanked him down.

"Hey!"

"Hey, yourself." She smiled up at him, looking immensely pleased with herself, then squeaked in surprise when he wrapped his arms around her and rolled so that she lay atop him, every sweet inch of her aligned with his own body.

"This is more like it," he pronounced.

"Umm-hmm." She wriggled her hips, effectively sandwiching his morning erection between them, and the feel of her silky flesh made him stiffen even more.

He groaned. "You're torturing me."

"No, I'm not." She propped herself up on his chest and circled one flat bronze nipple with her index finger.

"Yes, you are. I wasn't going to do anything this morning. I was going to be noble, let you have time to heal."

She dropped her head and licked his nipple experimentally with her tongue, and he almost jumped out of his skin with pleasure. "I don't need time to heal," she said in a husky voice.

He didn't need a second invitation. Rolling again, he switched their positions, then slid to one side so he could caress her warm, willing flesh.

In the early-morning light, her skin looked luminescent, as if it were lit from within by the smallest suggestion of light. He traced the line of her jaw, sliding over her heart-shaped chin and moving down her throat, stopping to lay his fingers over the place where her pulse fluttered beneath the fragile covering of skin. The flesh of her breasts was pale as porcelain, underlaid with a delicate webbing of blue veins.

He bent his head and gently kissed the closest nipple, then suckled lightly, feeling it draw into a tight bead beneath his attentions. Her fingers dug into his scalp. Repeating the action with the other breast, he used his fingers to roll and pluck at the sensitive tips. She was beginning to breathe faster, and she shifted her hips once on the bed. He doubted if she even knew she did it.

"Do you like that?" He raised his head to examine her face.

Her eyes were closed, but her lips curved up a bit at the corners and she breathed, "Yes."

He bent again to his task, until her chest was heaving and she clutched at his back and biceps with damp hands. "Please…"

"Please what?" His own flesh had responded to the scent and feel of her in its predictable way, and he surged against her hip once, trying to ignore the throbbing ache that begged him for release.

She grasped his wrist and swept it down across her body, whispering, "Touch me. Like you did before."

She had picked the damnedest time to remind him of *that*. He was so hard he actually hurt, but he forced his mind away from his pulsing flesh, spreading his fingers wide to comb through the nest of curls she'd directed him to. Her legs moved restlessly and she opened them the tiniest bit, inviting him in. With the lightest of caresses, he drew a single finger down, tracing the seam that lay between her legs, then retracing the path back up to circle lightly over the small nub he found at its beginning.

Her back arched. She rolled her hips and he used the

motion to place his palm against the shadowed cleft, bathing him in slippery, steaming heat. He groaned. She was ready. He could take her now without hurting her. He shifted over her, lay himself between her thighs and let the taut head of his swollen flesh rub gently against her. She moved her hips in a new way, helping him continue to please her, but he knew he wasn't going to be able to wait much longer if he stayed in this position, and he wanted her to enjoy it this time, so he started to move away again so that he could use his hand.

"No!" Her legs drew together around his hips, surprisingly powerful, holding him in place. "Don't stop."

"I don't want to hurt you," he panted.

She didn't answer but spread her legs and dug her heels into the mattress, sliding down so that she caught him with the clasp of her body. Poised to enter her, he used every ounce of self-control he possessed to move forward steadily, slowly, letting her feel his size as her body stretched and accepted him.

"What are you doing?" Her eyes were open now, and he could swear she sounded irritated.

"I'm trying…to take it…easy. I don't want…to hurt you again." Beneath his chest, her breasts pushed against him, making his own nipples tighten into tiny buds of need.

She dug her heels into his buttocks now, inexorably shoving him deep within her. "Don't wait. Please don't wait."

And suddenly, he couldn't. Not for another second. His hips flexed, sheathing him within her until they were pressed together, belly to belly. But he didn't take time to savor the sensation. He couldn't. His head pounded, blood rushing through it as his body began the primitive, driving rhythm that would lead him to climax. Her heels climbed his back as he thrust, and she threw her head back, her body arching like a drawn bow. A high keening tore from her throat as he felt the ripples of her release begin, shaking her like a leaf in a high wind and milking him in intense, repeated pulses that stroked the flesh fitted within her. At the back of his neck, a shiver began, working its way down his backbone in a lightning flash of command, and his body obeyed, taking him into his own frenzied, jolting, tooth-grinding finish.

When the storm passed, he wanted to do nothing more than close his eyes and sleep, right there on and in her. But perhaps she didn't. Dread coiled in his stomach as he raised himself over her and looked into her face. He hadn't meant to lose control like that. He'd hurt her again—

She was smiling.

Cautiously, he said, "You look…happy." *Happy* didn't cover it, though he wasn't about to tell her she looked wanton, satisfied.

Her smile grew wider. "You were right." Her hand moved from his back, sliding up to caress the fine hairs at the back of his neck.

"About?"

"It is easier after the first time."

"If it's done right, it should be. Otherwise, how would a man ever coax his woman back for more?"

She laughed, and it struck him that he was enjoying this as much as he did the sex. He'd never known this cozy intimacy before, and he liked it.

He liked it a lot.

Eight

The first thing she saw when she pulled into the driveway was Thad. He was mowing the grass in a pair of ragged cutoffs. His only other clothing was his sneakers, the old ratty ones that looked like they'd been through a war. She'd almost thrown them out last week, but he pitched a fit, insisting that they were the most comfortable shoes he owned for yard work. She guessed he hadn't been exaggerating.

He smiled when he saw her. She waved at him and went on into the trailer. Her knees were shaky and her pulse raced from no more than that wordless exchange. Lordy, what that man did to her system!

Surely it was sinful to lust after a man's body like this, even if he was your husband. She had walked around in a daze of sensuality throughout the whole past month. Even when she wasn't with him, her mind replayed vivid fantasies of their lovemaking, fantasies that made her body ache with need. At the office, her father had to speak twice before she heard him. It was embarrassing, darn it. If women didn't go into heat, then this must be the next thing to it.

Outside, she heard the mower cut off. She filled a glass with ice water and walked out the back door. Thad was standing in the shade of the big tree beside the trailer, mopping his face and chest with a T-shirt he must have discarded earlier.

"Ah-h-h. Thanks. It was hot today." He took the drink and lifted it to his lips. As he drank, the strong muscles in his neck worked, and she forced herself to look away. A woman could only take so much temptation.

"I guess I'd better start supper."

"Forget supper. It's too hot to eat." He grabbed her hand and began to pull her away from the house. "We can put a cold meal together when we come back."

"When we come back from where?" He was leading her into the woods behind the house, and she protested as she realized she was still wearing her office clothing. "Wait a minute. I have to change my clothes."

"Your clothes will be fine, I promise." He ignored the first question as he moved with easy familiarity down a well-marked path ahead of her.

It was a little bit cooler beneath the trees. She could hear water burbling somewhere nearby, and the full force of the late-day sun didn't penetrate the dense canopy of leaves. She gave up questioning and just followed him. She knew him well enough by now to know that she wouldn't get a single scrap of information out of him unless he chose to enlighten her.

The sound of water was very near now, and in another moment they emerged into a small clearing near the stream. Less than thirty feet from bank to bank, it meandered around a sharp curve at the place where they stood, creating a little point that sloped gently to the water's edge.

"Oh, this is pretty. I didn't even know this stream was back here." Though now that she thought about it, she realized it must be the Antietam Creek, which cut through the southern part of the county before wandering away into Maryland, passing through battlefields that had been saturated with blood almost a century and a half ago. She crossed it every day on her way into town, driving over a scenic stone bridge left from an earlier era.

"I've been coming down to this old swimming hole since I was a kid." Thad stopped on a grassy verge near the water's edge. He pried his sneakers off one at a time, balancing on the other leg like a big stork. "Nobody comes here anymore. There are other spots that are bigger and a lot easier to get to, I guess." His shoes removed, he placed his hands at the worn waistband of his jeans and opened the snap with a small popping sound. "Gonna take a dip with me?"

No wonder he'd been so sure her clothes would be all right. She stared at him, then at the water. Obviously he didn't expect her to *wear* any clothes.

"Um, I don't…think so." She couldn't imagine taking off her clothes outside. Just the thought made her feel exposed. She pointed to a large boulder a few feet away. "I'll just sit and relax over there."

Thad shrugged. His face was a blank mask; she had no idea what he was thinking. "You don't know what you're missing." Ignoring her completely, he shucked out of his jeans and briefs and walked toward the water.

She stared at him, dry-mouthed, as he waded into the

stream. Oh, yes. She knew exactly what she was missing. His shoulders were bronzed already from the sun. The breadth of them when he took off his shirt never failed to surprise her all over again. Her hands itched to stroke over those shoulders, to feel the play of the long, corded muscles of his legs, which flexed and shifted as he walked. His sex hung heavily against his thighs, cushioned in a thicket of hair as golden as that on his head.

They'd explored each other's bodies thoroughly in the weeks since the wedding, but she'd never watched him so openly before. In the trailer, no matter if they were in the bedroom or the kitchen or the tiny living room, she was a creature of sensation. She knew her way around his body blindfolded by now, but if he was in a nude line-up with a bag over his head, she wondered if she'd be able to pick out his body. The outrageous thought made her giggle, and he turned his head to survey her as he waded into the creek.

"Are you laughing at me?" He looked down at his body, definitely as unaroused as it could get in the cold water. "I guess it is pretty laughable."

"That's not it!" She was giggling openly now as she perched on the edge of the rock after giving the surface a cursory swipe with her hand to clear away any dirt.

"Well, if it isn't that, then what is it?"

"Nothing." No way on earth could she explain to him what she was thinking. In his arms she didn't feel shy very often anymore, but she still couldn't talk about sex without blushing. Which she was doing right now, darn it.

"The day a woman is thinking nothing is the day the world ends," he predicted darkly, just before he submerged himself in the deepest part of the stream, near the tree roots at the far side.

She propped herself back on her hands and tilted her face up to the sun, still warm during these long early-summer days. The water looked cool and tempting, and she would love to take a dip. Why not? But as much as she wanted to be the kind of woman who wouldn't worry about stripping off her clothes in broad daylight, she *would* worry. What if someone came by?

A splash caught her attention, and she saw Thad stroking through the rippling water, the muscles of his arms gleaming. She still couldn't believe she was married to him. She, Chloe Miller—Chloe Shippen, she corrected—could touch that gorgeous male splashing in the creek anytime she liked. It was like a dream from which she hadn't awakened.

A dream marred only by the knowledge that her husband liked her and desired her, but didn't love her.

A voice near her right side said, "The water feels great."

She sat up with a start, pressing her hand to her heart. "You scared me!" Her body sagged in the automatic relaxation produced by relief.

"Sorry." His grin flashed, white and insincere, as he crossed his arms on the edge of the rock and rested his chin on the back of one, allowing his body to float in the water. "So...what did you do today?"

She shrugged. "Same old, same old. Most of the records that we saved have been restored in the new computers."

"Are you enjoying it?"

She cast him a sideways glance that clearly asked after his sanity. "I'd rather be working with children. *That* would be a challenge I'd enjoy."

"We can remedy that in about nine months." He traced one wet finger from the inside of her knee up her inner thigh, brushing her skirt aside as his hand moved higher.

Children of their own. She wanted them, definitely, could almost see chubby little boys with golden hair tearing through the house. But she wasn't ready to change this idyllic time when just the two of them made their family complete. Before she brought children into the world, she was going to be sure their parents shared love.

His fingers found the edge of her panties and slowly explored, and she almost relaxed and let him touch her—and then she remembered where they were. She pressed her legs together, preventing him from any more intimate touch. What if someone came along and saw them? "Not here," she said. "I wasn't talking about our family and you know it."

"Right. You meant your preschool." Abruptly he removed his hand. "If it's so important to you, what are you waiting for? Quit your job and get started." His voice was cool, almost challenging, as he pushed off the rock and let the current carry him away from her.

She sat up and pulled her skirt over her knees, no longer enjoying the warmth of the day. Why had he gotten so distant all of a sudden? They'd been talking about her work, and all of a sudden he was cooler than iced tea. What had she said? Then it hit her. It wasn't what she had said, it was what she had done. He was miffed because she hadn't let him entice her into lovemaking out here by the stream.

He wasn't really interested in talking. When they were together, he was thinking about making love. Or recovering from making love. She'd known when she married him that he didn't love her the way she loved him, but she'd counted on proximity drawing them together, forging common bonds they shared.

As she stood and dusted off her skirt, she thought sadly that the only bonds they were forging were the physical kind. And much as she liked that, she needed more.

It's only been a month, she told herself. *Meaningful relationships take time to grow. Be patient.*

He watched her walking back up the trail to the house as he pulled his shorts on and stuffed his briefs in his pocket. What if she didn't want children at all? He knew her well enough to know that if she bore children, she'd never break up their marriage. Maybe she was afraid he wouldn't be a good father. Hell, he wondered that himself. It wasn't like he'd had a role model or anything.

He sprinted up the path. To hell with it. He was probably wasting a lot of good brain cells on this. Relationships never lasted a lifetime. He'd seen enough men come and go through his mother's life to know that monogamy—and love—were myths.

So what if he'd been thinking both were possible since he'd met her?

As he emerged from the woods, he could see her. She was almost back at the house. Her head was down, and she walked without her customary lilt.

What did she have to be upset about? Other than the fact that her damned school was still a dream.

Her father, surprisingly, didn't kick and scream like she thought he would when he read the letter of resignation she handed him at the end of the workday the next day.

"This was temporary. We both knew it," she said.

Reverend Miller snorted, though the sound was good-humored. "Some of us knew it faster than others." He laid the letter to one side. "I guess you're going to be busy soon enough, anyway."

"That's for sure. Did I tell you we think we've found a house? Thad's having a contractor look it over with him this afternoon. It's an old farmhouse. There's a shed behind the house that Thad can renovate for a workshop, and the kitchen is huge. It has two fireplaces and five bedrooms and—" she grimaced "—a bathroom that will have to be modernized before we do anything else!"

"That's good. You'll want to be moved in and organized before the baby comes."

"And I—*what did you say?*"

He only smiled at her. "It's all right. I've known since before the wedding."

She couldn't find her voice for a moment. This wasn't quite the kind of discussion she'd ever imagined having with her father, for heaven's sake! Finally she managed to speak. "You think I'm pregnant?"

"I'm delighted," he assured her.

"You're delighted. And the fact that you assume I got into this condition before the wedding doesn't bother you?"

"I was very disappointed." He shot her a stern look over the tops of his glasses. "You had strong moral guidelines that I had hoped —"

"Well, it bothers me! I am *not* pregnant." She stopped, feeling sheepish. "Well, I could be, now, but I wasn't when we got married."

Her father's brows rose in question. "You weren't? But when Thad came to see me, he said—"

"Thad came to see you?" she repeated. "When was this?"

"When he came to ask me for your hand."

"He *asked* you for my hand?" She was overwhelmed by facts that didn't compute. This whole conversation was beginning to make her feel like Alice must have felt when she first saw the Mad Hatter race by.

"Well, strictly speaking, he didn't ask. He told me that you were marrying, and he asked me to help plan the ceremony."

"And he told you I was pregnant?" She was going to have quite a chat with Thad. And while she chatted, she was going to pull out every soft, curling hair on his chest, one by one by one.

"Actually, he said you needed to be married right away. I suppose I assumed…but he definitely wanted me to believe—"

"I see."

"So I'm not going to be a grandfather yet?"

"Not yet." Her face felt frozen; she had to consciously relax her jaw. "I have to go. I'll write a job description for you as soon as I get a chance."

Her drive home to the trailer was fueled by fury. It was almost dinnertime, but when she pulled into the driveway, she didn't see his truck. She slammed drawers and banged pans as she threw together a casserole for dinner. What reason could he possibly have had for leading her father to conclude… Oh, thinking about it just made her angry all over again. She tossed the casserole into the oven and was heading for the bedroom to change her clothes when the door swung open.

Thad stepped into the room, and the small interior of their home immediately seemed even tinier.

"Hello," he said, reaching for her. "We have a green

light on the hou— Hey!'' He grabbed her wrists as she shoved against his chest.

It had been almost a reflex; she hadn't been expecting him right at that moment, and when he'd walked right into her path, she hadn't wanted to be touched. ''You…you rotten, lying *rat.*'' It was the worst insult she could come up with. ''Why did you make my father think I was pregnant?''

He stared at her as if she'd gone mad. Which probably wasn't too far from the truth. Slowly he straightened away from the door, keeping his eyes on her. ''I didn't lie to him,'' he said. ''He jumped to that conclusion all by himself.''

''Don't you split hairs with me.'' She stepped forward again and poked him in the chest. ''You *led* him to believe we had to get married fast, and then you *allowed* him to keep believing it. You knew how important it was to me to come to my marriage, *untouched,* and now my own father is going to think I didn't—I wasn't—''

''You *didn't* come to this marriage untouched.'' His tone was angry, too. ''The way I remember it, I touched you pretty damn near everywhere before I ever put a ring on your finger. And you enjoyed it.''

She ground her teeth together so hard she'd probably damaged the enamel. ''Thank you so much for reminding me. I forgot what a *gentleman* you are.'' She started to brush by him, intending to go back to the bedroom and grandly slam the door in his face and stay there for the rest of the evening, but he reached out and caught her by the arm.

''Let go of me!'' She tried to wrench her arm away, but he used both hands to wrestle her up against his body, holding her wrists behind her in one hand and roughly taking her chin in the other.

"If you're going to be mad at me, I may as well give you something to be mad about."

She twisted, trying to wrench her head away as he set his mouth down on hers but he simply hitched her higher against his body and lifted her off her feet. One of her kicking feet caught him solidly on the shin, and he grunted, lifting his head.

They glared at each other for a few taut seconds. She was furious with him. She really was. But her body, pressed intimately against his and coursing with adrenaline, communicated another message. Between them, his growing length told her that he was as aroused as she suddenly was. Heat pooled between her legs, and she felt herself going soft and wet. She struggled to remember why she was angry, but her mind drew a blank. His expression changed, and his gaze dropped to her lips. She could swear she felt him touching her.

This time when he lowered his head, she didn't try to get away. Her mouth clung to his and her tongue met him, demanding more. He had set her back on her feet, and she lifted one leg, wrapping it around the back of his thigh and rubbing herself against him. He released her hands and grasped her buttocks in both big palms. She hadn't started a fight with this result in mind, but she couldn't wait for his possession. Reaching for him, she ripped at the buttons on his shirt, and he glanced down in astonishment as one popped off and flew across the room. Then, almost instantly, her urgency communicated itself to him. He burrowed under her skirt, lifting handfuls of fabric out of the way until he could reach her. Stripping her panty hose and the panties beneath them down her legs, he peeled the hose away until she could kick out of them. She was fumbling with the front of his trousers and he shoved her hands aside, opening his jeans and freeing himself from the briefs beneath. She grasped him in one small hand, murmuring with pleasure, and he groaned. He couldn't wait long enough to take her to the bedroom. He had to have her *now*. He lifted her by the waist, turning so that she was braced against the door. He didn't bother removing the skirt, and she lifted it out of the way, then clutched at his shoulders as he used his body to spread her legs wide, entering her in one mighty thrust.

Her back arched, and she yanked his head up to hers by simply pulling on his hair; her mouth was ferocious. He held her in place against the door, silently thrusting in and out of her as their mouths mated. She felt like her skin was electrified, every sensation magnified by her heightened emotions. She loved the feel of him between her legs, his body pounding against her most sensitive flesh, his tongue matching the rhythm of his hips. Abruptly she realized her body was beginning its surge toward satisfaction. She could feel her climax gathering into a tight fist within her, only to explode, shattering her into shards of mindless sensation. She tore her mouth away from his, crying out as her body shuddered and bucked against him. He didn't let her rest but continued his assault, baring his teeth in what might have been a smile. "My turn."

Her body was so sensitive that she felt as if she'd received an electric shock with each stroke of his flesh, each meeting of his torso against hers. She cried out as, incredibly, she felt herself rushing to a second peak, and he gave an involuntary groan as his body stiffened and shook, surging against her in the throes of his own climax.

When he was finished, they both hung against the door, chests heaving. She reached up and caught a drop of sweat with her thumb as it trickled down his temple. He staggered to the couch, slipping from her body as they sat, and sank down with a grateful sigh. His legs couldn't have carried him another step. Chloe lay on his chest, her breath coming hard and fast against his neck, and despite the lethargy that invited him to simply drop his head back and close his eyes, he lifted his arms and wrapped them around her, holding her close as their breathing steadied and their pulses returned to a less frantic rhythm.

He stroked a hand down her hair, a chuckle rumbling up from the depths of his chest. "I vote we always fight like that."

Her lips curved into a smile against his neck. "Was that our first fight?"

He shrugged, running his palms up and down her slender back. "You prefer *disagreement?*"

She brushed the tips of her fingers lightly across the hairs on his chest, and he felt ripples of goose bumps spring up. "I don't know what to call it." Sitting up on his lap, she gave him a long, sober look. "I'm sorry I shouted at you." She shook her head. "I don't know what happened. I just got so *mad.*"

He sighed. "I'm sorry, too. I shouldn't have implied that to your father."

"Why did you?" She didn't sound angry anymore, just curious.

He hesitated. How could he explain the compulsion that had driven him? *I was afraid you wouldn't want to marry me if you had time to think about it?* He settled for "I wanted you too much to wait."

She didn't say anything in answer, simply lifted her

hand to his cheek, but he noticed she didn't meet his eyes.

Turning his head, he kissed her palm. "Am I forgiven?"

She nodded. "It doesn't really matter what my father believes. I just hate the idea of people thinking you took advantage of me, when we both know that's not true."

Deep in his chest, the icy sense of unease thawed. As usual, she was more concerned with what people thought of him than she was of herself. It sounded as if she was planning on being with him for the long haul. It was a pleasing thought.

"This isn't great, but I can live with it for a while." Chloe stood in the middle of the kitchen in the house they'd just bought. They'd signed the final papers that morning. It had given her a warm feeling to see her name underneath Thad's on the deed. A good feeling.

She looked around the enormous old room. It hadn't been renovated for at least fifty years. There were no counters, few cupboards, and the sink was one of the wide, shallow kind that she'd seen in some of their oldest parishioners' homes.

"You don't have to live with it at all," Thad said. "We can afford to renovate the upstairs bathroom, put one in down here and still redo the kitchen. The rest of it, we can work on ourselves."

She shifted, uncomfortable with the idea of him using all his savings on the house. "I really don't mind waiting. We can set aside a little bit at a time for—"

"Chloe."

Her name on his lips stopped the flow of words.

"What's bothering you? I want to get this all done at one time. The thought of living with workmen traips-

ing in and out for months on end doesn't appeal to me."
He crossed the floor to her, placing his arms around her
waist and pulling her back against him. Bending his
head, he blew a warm stream of air against the spot
right behind her ear that he'd discovered got to her
every time, and, as always, she relaxed, letting her body
soften against him in surrender.

"I feel *funny,* using your money for all this."

"It's not *my* money. It's *our* money."

His lips nibbled down the side of her neck, and a
wave of heat rushed through her. "Thad, wait!"

She could feel him smile against her skin. "For what?
We're alone for the first time in our house. Don't you
think we ought to celebrate?"

"Seems to me we've celebrated an awful lot since
we got married." She was smiling now, too. His lovemaking was as fierce and devastating each time he
touched her as it had been from the beginning. In his
arms, she became someone new even to herself, matching his passion with her own. She floated through her
days waiting for evening and his return home, feeling
as if she were only half alive until he walked through
the door and touched her.

"We have a lot to celebrate," he said in her ear.
"Your last day at the church is tomorrow. Then you
can work on the house to your heart's content."

"While I work on my preschool proposal."

"Whatever. You know you don't have to work. If
you want to be home with the children, I can support
us."

Children. Another troubling thought. But his words
reminded her of something. "Um, we can't "celebrate"
for a few days. I found out this morning that I'm not
pregnant."

His hands stilled in their exploration of her body, then slowly dropped away from her. "All right. Let me know when—"

"Okay," she said hastily. Her body suddenly felt chilled. Was it unreasonable of her to want to be cuddled even when they couldn't make love? *He didn't marry you for love,* she reminded herself with brutal honesty. *He married you for your body.* Thad had seemed a little reserved, a bit distant for the past few weeks. The only time she felt like he was completely with her was when they were making love. Which, she acknowledged, was almost all the time when they were together.

He already had stepped away from her and was looking critically around the kitchen. "Why don't we talk about what we'd like the finished room to be like."

As he began to tell her about traffic patterns and the triangle that made the best workspace, she felt her enthusiasm fall away. "You decide what will work best. I'm sure I'll like it."

Thad accompanied her to church on Sunday as he'd done every week since the first time she had brought him. Outside, it was a glorious June day, but inside the church where the congregation was still meeting, it was sticky. By the time her father's sermon ended, women were fanning themselves with their bulletins and the men's starched shirts were wilting.

As Chloe preceded Thad out of the pew, a wave of dizziness rushed up over her. She clutched at the corner of the pew for support, but the world continued to spin. Thad caught her by the elbow.

"What's the matter?"

"I'm a little dizzy," she said.

He put his arm around her and drew her back into the pew.

"Sit down."

She did, and immediately began to feel a bit better.

"How about some water?" Thad was hovering over her.

"That would be nice," she replied, more to give him something to do than because she really wanted a drink.

"Stay right there. Don't try to get up until I get back."

"Okay, boss."

It was evident that he wasn't amused, by the dark look he cast her before he turned away.

She watched him sprint out of the rapidly emptying sanctuary. She just didn't understand him. He was solicitous in public, passionate in private. But since their marriage, he'd avoided sharing any personal moments.

"What's the matter, dear?"

She turned to see one of the other parishioners bearing down on her. "Nothing," she said. "Or not much. I felt a little dizzy, so Thad went to get me a drink. It's just this heat."

"It certainly is hot." The matron fanned herself vigorously. Then she leaned forward, focusing on Chloe's hands. "I never did get to see your engagement ring, dear."

Chloe sighed inwardly. Another busybody. "I don't have one," she said. "But my wedding band is lovely. Thad picked it out himself." She shoved her ring finger under the lady's nose.

"It's just darling! My, weren't you a surprise. I don't believe anyone even knew you were dating seriously, and here you go off and get married!"

Chloe smiled.

The woman looked a bit disconcerted at this lack of response. She released Chloe's hand. "Of course, we all wish you the very best." Her voice dropped to a whisper. "I knew his first wife. Poor little thing. I hope you have better luck than she did."

Chloe sat up a little straighter. "Mrs. Goode, I'm surprised at you." She pitched her voice to carry just a little, so that the only people who could hear her were the ones in danger of spraining their necks trying to eavesdrop. "If that's your way of expressing your congratulations on my marriage, then perhaps you shouldn't say anything at all."

The woman's face was as red as a fat, juicy tomato. "I...I—"

As soon as the words had left her mouth, Chloe had felt bad. Gently, she tried to soften her tone. "I come into this place of worship to unburden myself of the unkind things I say and do. I have trouble sometimes with not judging others, but it's a flaw I try to work on. I'm sure you do, too." She smiled directly into the woman's eyes, willing herself to let go of her annoyance and heed her own words.

Mrs. Goode had recovered her aplomb by the time Chloe finished speaking. "Sounds as if your father isn't the only preacher in this congregation. You've missed your calling, young lady. I apologize." But there was a twinkle in her eye and she was smiling as she turned away.

"Chloe." Thad's voice startled her, and she turned to find him standing behind her. He'd come up the other side of the aisle. "Here's your water."

She smiled at Thad. "I feel better. I'm ready to go home."

Thad's mouth was compressed into a tight, angry

line. What in the world was the matter? He hadn't heard her exchange with Mrs. Goode, she hoped. She didn't linger to chat with anyone else, but headed directly for the parking lot, aware that the wrong word could cause an explosion.

He didn't speak all the way home. After he parked the car beside the trailer, he killed the engine before turning to her. "Do you still feel dizzy?" It was more a demand than a question.

"No." She looked at him wonderingly.

"Good." With that he slammed his door shut and mounted the step to the house with a leashed tension coiled in him so tightly she could see it from where she sat.

He was in the house before she even left the car.

What was wrong with *him?* Chloe unfastened her seat belt, struggling to control her own rising ire. Even if he was furious with Mrs. Goode, he shouldn't be taking it out on her. Besides, she was sure the woman hadn't meant to be cruel. She simply hadn't considered the brashness of her words.

She headed for the bedroom. Thad was just pulling a worn T-shirt over his head when she entered.

"I'm going out to the shop," he muttered, brushing by her. "I have some work to do."

"I thought we were going to start papering the walls in the dining room at the new house."

"It'll have to wait."

Wait? *Wait?* "Are you going to tell me what your problem is, or do I have to guess?" she inquired, sarcasm coating each syllable.

Halfway down the stairs, he whirled.

"I know I've made some stupid mistakes in my life. But I've paid for them and paid for them, and I'm damn sick of it! I don't care what other people think. And I don't need you to defend me!''

"You never objected to it before. I thought that was exactly why you married me." She was hurt beyond belief at his words, and angry now, too. How was she supposed to know that had bothered him? It was human nature—well, *her* nature, anyhow—to help anything in distress.

"Maybe it was! Is that any worse than you marrying me because you were too hot to wait?''

His words were so unfair they staggered her, slicing a deep gash in her heart. She was stunned, groping for a response. Before she could come up with something coherent, he was gone, slamming down the steps and out the back door.

Nine

The words that had been thrown between them hung in the air around her, a thick, black cloud that obscured her vision. Or maybe it was the tears that had begun to flow, regardless of how hard she pressed the heels of her palms against her eyes.

She groped for the edge of the bed and sank down, shaking. His words had shattered the illusion of normalcy she'd woven around their marriage. She'd told herself over and over again that he would come to love her, that there had to be something more than simple physical attraction between them, that they could build a life together.

But she'd been wrong. If only she'd had more experience, been more worldly. She would have known not to mistake simple chemistry for love. He'd told her he wanted her too much to wait through a long engagement, and she'd dared to hope he meant it in a deeper sense than the physical.

She'd thought they'd been sharing themselves with each other, while he'd been resenting every minute they spent together outside the bedroom.

Throwing herself down on the bed, she sobbed for what felt like hours, releasing all her hurt and disappointment. When she finally got herself under control, she knew she couldn't stay with him any longer. Their marriage had been a mistake that she would remember for the rest of her life. *The rest of her life without Thad.*

The thought brought more tears to her smarting, swollen eyes. Going to the closet, she pulled a suitcase out and opened it on the bed, then set about packing as many of her things as she could fit into it. Fortunately a lot of her possessions were still at her father's house, packed up and waiting to be moved into the new house.

"Where you lodge, I will lodge...."

Unbidden, the words of her wedding vows whispered through the room. Her hands stilled among the folded clothes.

Her head drooped, and she sank to the floor. What was she thinking? Thad was her husband now. She'd chosen him of her own free will. She couldn't run back to her father's house simply because her marriage wasn't working out the way she had hoped.

"Until death do us part."

That pretty much said it all. Slowly, she began to return clothing to drawers. Refusing to allow herself to replay the hurtful words he'd flung at her, she emptied the suitcase and returned it to the closet. She was married. That was all she needed to remember.

And if the love she had brought to the union wasn't enough to nourish their relationship, then she would live with the consequences of her hasty actions for the rest of her life. "Marry in haste, repent at leisure." It might be an old cliché, but whoever said it first said it perfectly.

Blowing her nose one final time, she went to the kitchen. She was going to prepare lunch. After that she was going over to the new house and start wallpapering the dining room. While she worked, she could compose a letter to several area churches and recreation centers asking about the possibility of starting a preschool.

"You don't know a damn thing—"

No! Don't think about it.

Let's see, she'd need a letter to the local businessmen asking for sponsorship for the first year or two until the program began to pay for itself. The furniture, toys and supplies would have to be outright donations....

He stayed in the workshop until early evening, until his stomach was growling. What was the point in going back into the house? Chloe had climbed into her car and left about an hour after he'd ruined any chance he'd ever had of keeping her. He'd noticed from the workshop window that she didn't take any bags with her, but it didn't make him feel much better. He knew she had left plenty of her own things at her father's home. She wouldn't be back.

And it was all his fault. He'd wanted her, been determined to have her, from the first time he'd seen her perching on that little chair with such ladylike posture in her office at the church. Her skirt had ridden up a little, but she hadn't pulled it down because she didn't think there was anyone else around, and he'd practically had to wipe drool from his chin looking at those long, slender legs and her pretty feet slipped into high heels. Did she have any idea how sexy those shoes were?

She did now. The thought was sobering, crushing. He'd pursued her, pestered her, petted her until he'd caught her. He'd taught her everything she knew about her own passionate nature, about responding to a man.

And he had driven her away. He'd known from the beginning that she was too good for him, that it couldn't last. He'd heard it spoken aloud time after time, heard her defending him—and he had taken out his frustration on her.

Other men would take one look and pursue her just like he had. And when she made a new life for herself with one of them, another man would be fixing up a home with her, sitting beside her in church, sharing stolen kisses over a picnic lunch.

Another man would realize he didn't want babies quite yet, because he wasn't ready to share her, even with their children. Another man would be holding her close at night, loving her, thanking his lucky stars she loved him and cherishing her the way she deserved to be cherished.

Cherishing her...loving her...loving her just like he did.

If he hadn't just used the last board he had in stock, he would have hit himself over the head with a two-by-four.

He hadn't allowed himself to even think it before, hadn't allowed the word *love* to surface in his mind. Sex was sex. Love was love. Great sex didn't mean lasting love. He'd had plenty of practice observing *that* little axiom. He would have died before telling anyone he was in love. Even the woman he loved.

But now...now, it didn't seem so important to hold

on to his pride and his independence. Not when the only woman he'd ever wanted to spend his life with had slipped through his grasp.

Slowly he replaced his tools and swept the floor before heading for the house. The silence inside the trailer seemed dark and oppressive. He flipped on the light in the kitchen, half expecting to see a note.

No note. And none in the bedroom, the only other logical place she would have placed it.

His stomach growled, reminding him it was feeding time. He put the remains of the chicken-corn soup Chloe had made in a bowl and nuked it while he peeled an orange and ate it standing at the sink. He was just checking to see if the soup was ready, when he heard her car crunch into the gravel of the driveway. Her car! Was he hallucinating?

Nope. She parked and got out. Her clothes were dirty and she had a hole in the knee of her pants.

As she dragged herself to the door, he saw her wince, and he had it open before she could reach for the knob. Had she been in an accident? "What the hell happened to you?"

She glanced at him quickly, then looked away. But he'd seen wariness in that glance and knew he deserved it. Why was she here after the things he'd said?

"I was wallpapering." She said it in a matter-of-fact tone, and before he could absorb that, she wandered over to the microwave and peeked into the bowl. "Mmm. Smells good. Did I miss supper?"

He shook his head, mimicking her casual tone, because he wasn't sure how to respond. "I was just getting ready to eat. I'll set two places."

"I can mix up some biscuits and throw a salad together."

What was going through her head? She was perfectly pleasant, and she actually smiled at him as she washed her hands. It was a fake smile, not her usual warm one, but at least she was looking at him.

He didn't know what was going on, but he didn't want her to leave again. He searched for something neutral to say, but couldn't come up with anything brilliant. "You sit. I'll make biscuits and salad."

"Oh, thanks." She sank into a chair with a grateful sigh. "I got almost two walls of the dining room done. Tomorrow I might be able to finish it. Wait till you see it—the paint looks fantastic with the paper. I'm glad you insisted on the lighter color."

Whatever she was thinking, she was offering a peace pipe and he grabbed at it. "I've learned from my own mistakes that paint always looks darker than the sample chips."

They didn't speak much throughout the meal. Beneath her surface calm, he sensed something unsettled, something wary. He could understand that.

But she seemed determined not to mention anything personal. Why? He wanted to ask her, to apologize for the hurt he'd put in her eyes earlier, but the woman before him wasn't the kind a guy could apologize to. If he tried now, his words would slide right off the slick surface of the wall she'd built around herself.

When the food was gone, she stood. He noticed how carefully she moved, and guilt pricked at him again. If he'd helped her with the papering like he'd promised, she wouldn't have worked herself so hard.

"I'm going to take a hot bath," she said. "You can leave the dishes in the sink, and I'll do them after breakfast."

But he didn't. While she was in the bathroom, he

cleaned up the kitchen, then turned on a ballgame. The Orioles were ahead by two runs, but they were struggling to hold on to that lead. It was a tense game, the kind the fans loved—and he had to force himself to watch it. Every two minutes he checked his watch.

She must really be sore, he thought, thirty minutes later. She would turn into a prune if she stayed in the water much longer.

When thirty more minutes had passed, he couldn't stand it anymore. He went to the closed bathroom door. "Chloe?"

No answer.

He turned the knob, half-expecting that she had locked him out, but the door opened easily. "What are you—"

The room was humid and warm. Chloe lay in the small bathtub—sound asleep. His heart twisted as he looked at her features, soft in sleep and utterly relaxed. She was so beautiful, so perfect. If she left him, nothing in his life would be right, ever again.

He bent over the tub and called her name. When her eyelids fluttered, he said, "Put your arms around my neck." Automatically, more asleep than awake, she obeyed. As he lifted her out of the water, he stood her on her feet long enough to snag a bath sheet and bundle it around her. Her pretty breasts flattened as he wound the towel around her, but he wouldn't allow himself to linger over the soft curves. Then, regardless of the water that was soaking into his own clothing, he lifted her again and carried her into the bedroom.

She didn't resist when he unwrapped her from the towel and laid her in their bed, covering her before he turned away to lock the door and turn off all the lights. But when he had shed his own clothes and slipped into bed beside her, he hesitated. They'd fallen asleep in the position she called spoons since their first night together, but he didn't feel free to touch her tonight. Or maybe it was that he wanted to respect her space, if that was what she needed.

She already had turned onto her side facing away from him, as usual. Reaching out, he touched a hand to her waist. She immediately scooted back against him, and a warm rush of relief filled him. He pillowed her head on one arm and draped the other over her, flattening his palm over her stomach and pulling her snugly against him. As always the feel of her silky warmth made him hard and ready, but he ignored his arousal.

She couldn't possibly miss it, lying as she was with her buttocks pressed against his thighs, but she didn't acknowledge him. In any case, he couldn't imagine any less likely time to start lovemaking.

He just wanted to hold her.

She dreamed he was making love to her. His clever tongue teased the sensitive spot behind her ear. His fingers plucked and rolled her nipples; his hands stroked her all over. As his lips moved down her neck, his hand slipped between her thighs, preparing her for his entry, and she willingly opened, welcoming him into her body.

But then, before she could begin to enjoy the intimate coupling, his voice shattered the quickening silence.

"I married you for sex."

She began to cry, hot, scalding tears that rapidly pooled on the floor and made a small lake of the bedroom—

"Chloe? Come on, honey, wake up."

Gradually her mind began to grasp at reality as the dream world receded. She opened her eyes to find Thad leaning over her with a concerned look on his face. He raised a hand to her cheek and stroked his thumb across her skin. "What's wrong?"

She realized she was crying. That part hadn't been a dream. She struggled into a sitting position and reached for a tissue. "Nothing. I just had a bad dream."

"Want to tell me about it?"

Yes, she wanted to say. She wanted him to laugh and tell her how silly it was, that he loved her, that he had married her because he needed her on all levels, not just for physical release. But he hadn't, and she knew he didn't really want to hear about her nightmare. "No, but thank you for your concern."

He went still for a moment, then said, "Okay," but he didn't lie back down.

She sat for another minute, crumpling her tissue into a small, soggy wad, then set it aside. But as she began to recline, Thad put a hand on her arm. When she turned toward him, he slipped his arms around her and pulled her down, cradling her against the hard planes of his chest. His embrace held her closely to him, her head tucked under his chin. Their legs tangled; against her belly she could feel him stirring, growing to full tumescent arousal.

"Stop." She pushed at his chest. "I can't—tonight."

"It's all right. I just want to hold you."

"You never 'just want to hold me.'" Her voice wasn't angry, just weary.

Seven small words. He opened his mouth to deny their truth—and stopped, speechless as he recognized the accuracy of her remark. He'd been so busy protecting himself that he'd never thought of how his actions seemed to her.

Cautiously, he said, "I do now."

No response.

Finally she made a small sound, a mere sigh of breath. Her body relaxed against his, and he realized how tense she'd been holding herself. He wanted to talk, but he sensed she wasn't ready to listen. If he made so much as a peep, she'd tense up, clam up, maybe even *get up* and leave for good this time. Although she hadn't spoken in an accusatory tone a moment ago, he felt as if he were treading on a very narrow ledge; a single misstep would dislodge him. And he knew if he fell, he'd never manage to reclaim the ground he'd lost.

The morning sun was heating the bedroom to an uncomfortable temperature when he awoke the next morning. He knew before he opened his eyes that he was alone.

Chloe wasn't in the kitchen, but there was a fresh pot of coffee waiting for him. On the table was half a grapefruit, already sectioned the way he like them best, and a plate with several slices of the cinnamon bread she had made. He sniffed the pleasing aromas absently, wondering where she could be. Then a flash of movement outside caught his attention and he saw her, kneeling in the flowerbed beside the mailbox. It looked like she was trimming around the edges of the bed.

Why was she bothering with that when they would be moving in a few weeks? He eyed her lithe shape as he wolfed down cinnamon bread and sipped at coffee that was entirely too hot to drink in big gulps. Would she treat him with the same careful courtesy that she had last night? All things considered, he thought he'd rather have her scream and throw things. At least he knew how to respond to that.

When he'd cleaned up his dishes, he opened the door and stepped out into the June sunshine.

"Good morning." She turned and waved an arm in his general direction before turning back to her work.

"Good morning." He ambled across the lawn. "You got an early start today."

"I woke up early and couldn't get back to sleep, so I thought I might as well be useful."

A vivid image of what they usually did when they woke up early drifted into his mind. From the blush that was creeping up her neck, she was thinking of the same thing. His body stirred at the thought of those lazy, sensual morning encounters, and he quickly banished the thoughts. He didn't need sex complicating what he wanted to say to her this morning.

But as he looked down at her hands, he realized he didn't want to talk out here, where she could pretend to be busy or distracted. He extended his hand. "Would you take a walk with me?"

She glanced up at him again, squinting in the bright light as she rose to her feet and dusted off her hands against the old shorts she wore. "All right." She hesitated for such a brief moment that he might have missed it if he were less tuned in to her, then took the hand he was offering.

Satisfaction coursed through him at the feel of her small, soft palm sliding against his. He spread his fingers wide and linked them with hers before she could initiate a less intimate clasp.

He didn't really have a destination in mind. He just wanted her undivided attention. As they crossed the backyard and turned onto the wooded path leading to the old swimming hole, he was uncomfortably aware of the invisible shield she had erected around herself. She was with him, but not with him.

They walked for a few minutes in silence, until the glint of sun on water told them they were approaching the clearing where he'd tried to entice her into swimming nude.

He cleared his throat. "I owe you an apology."

"No, you don't." She smiled at him impersonally.

"Well, then, just pretend I'm doing this for fun," he said testily.

"I'd rather not." She broke free of his hand and headed for the water, stooping down to test it with her fingers. "It feels great. Let's go swimming."

"I don't think—" He broke off, his voice failing him at the sight of his wife unbuttoning the sleeveless blouse she wore. Before he could oil his vocal cords enough to make a sound, she had stepped out of every stitch of clothing she wore. "What are you doing?"

"Going swimming." Her tone was casual but he noted that she glanced around nervously. This wasn't as easy for her as she wanted him to believe. As she waded into the stream, he decided that her back view was as enticing as the front. A long, slim line marked by the slight ridge of her spine stretched from her slender neck to the heart-shaped curve of her bottom. The skin there was pale as porcelain and he knew from experience how soft it would feel under his hands. He could feel himself getting aroused; for once he was annoyed rather than amused at the effect she had on his senses. Dammit! He wanted to clear the air. To apologize for his unreasonable anger yesterday and hear her say she had forgiven him. He *needed* to hear her say it.

"Whew! It's chilly." She splashed on in until she

was submerged up to her neck. "Once you're wet it feels great. C'mon in."

It was almost funny. He'd dreamed about having her naked in the old swimming hole, been disappointed when she'd been too inhibited last time—and now he was the one who didn't want to take off his clothes. Reluctantly, his hands went to his belt.

She didn't watch him enter the water, but turned and swam upstream with a strong, steady crawl. It struck him that they knew so little about each other; he hadn't even known if she could swim. Maybe she was right about the kid thing. They *did* need a little time together before they enlarged their family.

She had flipped over onto her back and let the current carry her slowly downstream. As she reached the spot where he stood, he caught her by one ankle and pulled her toward him. The movement of the water pushed her toward him and she spread her legs and caught him around the waist. The sudden shock of her soft woman's flesh pressed against his abdomen ignited a fire deep in his belly. Looking down, he saw her soft brown nest of curls mingling with his own bush of hair; heat raced through him. He could feel himself quickening, pulsing, no longer minding the water's temperature, growing harder and harder until his aroused flesh brushed against her buttocks. She was pink and white and pretty, framed by the cool water rippling around her, and her breasts were buoyant, bobbing gently as if begging for his attention.

He had automatically put his arms around her back to support her; she linked her hands behind his neck and pulled his head down, thrusting her breasts at him.

"Wait." He resisted her with the last of his strength. "We need to talk."

She laughed, and it was the siren's song that had lured men for centuries. "No, we don't. We need to do something about this."

Using the weightlessness the water provided, she slipped away from him far enough to capture his erection against her. He gasped, a harsh sound of shock and pleasure, and he was lost.

He thrust himself into her in one long stroke, and the heat of her body compared to the coolness of the water seared him. Forcing himself to hold still within her despite the urgency licking at his nerve endings, he let her guide his mouth to her breast. She liked to be touched there, he knew, and he suckled, circled and fondled until she was writhing against him and his body wouldn't let him be still any longer. Gripping her hips, he started to move, but the weight and motion of the water slowed him too much. She uttered a sound of dismay and he put his mouth on hers, kissing her deeply as he began to make his way toward the creek bank. Without releasing her or himself, he surged toward the bank, coming down with her onto the sweet, spongy grass at the water's edge. Their legs were still in the water but he was blind to everything other than her. His world was beneath him, around him, hot and tight and matching the frantic pace he set. She lifted her hips to him over and over, and he looked down at her face. She was close, he could tell, her breath rushing in and out and her cheeks flushed with color. Her eyes were open, watching him, and he held the contact, deepening the intimacy. Gripping her bottom with both hands, he angled her up higher and doubled his rhythm.

Never taking her gaze from his, she whimpered and jerked as her climax rolled over her, and he groaned, giving in to his own release as her inner pulses squeezed his swollen length. It seemed forever that she milked him; when it was finished he dropped his head and let his weight settle slowly onto hers as his chest heaved and his heart rate steadied. Finally they were both quiet. Her hands smoothed gently over his back, sliding down over his buttocks. He propped himself up just enough to see her face, then dropped his head and kissed her. "My campaign must have been successful."

"What?"

"I voted for ending all our fights like this, remember?" He smiled down at her.

And just that fast, she was gone. The warm, willing woman with the intimate smile who lay beneath him, still harboring him within her, became the cool, friendly but not approachable woman she'd been since she returned last night. And equally fast, his patience vanished. He wasn't going to let her shut him out again, dammit.

"Hello in there. Anybody home?"

Her gaze came back to his, clearly startled. "I beg your pardon?"

God, he loved the way that phrase rolled off her tongue. He was tempted to give her permission to beg, but he had something other than a double entendre on his mind today. "You were a million miles away. Where did you go?"

"Nowhere." She shrugged, and the movement of her silken shoulder caused one breast to slide up and down against his chest. Delightful as the sensation was, he wasn't going to let himself be distracted this time.

"Yes, you did. You've been putting me on one of your mental shelves since you came home last night. I want to know why."

"I'm sorry." Her voice was quiet and even.

He gritted his teeth. "Don't be sorry. Be truthful."

"I'm not lying!"

The flash of irritation was the first real emotion he'd seen, other than the way she'd lost herself in lovemaking. "I didn't say you were. If you're still mad about yesterday, just come out and say it."

"I'm not mad." She looked away. "I was hurt, at first, but I'd rather know how you really feel than be walking around in a daze, thinking we have a normal marriage."

"I'm sorry I yelled at you." He caressed the ball of her shoulder and traced a line across her collarbone. "I didn't mean what I said. You know how much your 'running interference' for me has helped. I was fed up with people always forcing you to defend me, and mad at myself for being the kind of man you have to defend."

Then the rest of what she'd said penetrated. "What do you mean by that crack about us not having a normal marriage? It seems pretty normal to me."

Beneath him, she sighed, and he lifted his weight onto his elbows more fully so she wasn't uncomfortable. He was vividly aware of their joined bodies, pleasantly so, but it suddenly occurred to him that making love to her might not be the same act in her mind that it was in his. The thought chilled him. He might not have said the words, but surely she could tell how much he cared by the way he treated her, by the way he touched her.

Couldn't she?

"Don't pretend you don't know what I mean, Thad." At least her indifference had vanished. "We got married for one reason."

"Well maybe you'd better clue me in," he said, uneasiness beginning to writhe deep within him.

He was so close that he clearly read the decision in her eyes, and a cold foreboding dimpled his arms with gooseflesh. He'd wanted to know what she was thinking, and he was about to have his wish granted.

Chloe hesitated. Thad's body had gone stiff and angry on hers; she could feel the thin control he had on the imminent explosion of his temper as he pulled away from her and sat up. She sat up, too, hugging her knees to her chest and looking out over the water. Before, she would have been terrified that someone might come along and see them. Today...well, today, worrying about what someone else might think was beyond her.

But she might as well be truthful. She would tell him everything—except that she loved him so much it destroyed her to think of leaving, even when she knew he didn't return her love. That just sounded too pitiful to put into words.

Taking a deep breath, she said, "You told me when you asked me to marry you that you couldn't wait any longer. I knew when I accepted, that...sex...was important to you. That if I wanted to be with you, we'd have to get married."

He rolled away from her and sat up, then turned and looked at her, and she felt scorched by the sizzling anger in his blue eyes. "And you think that's the only reason I asked you to marry me?"

She didn't really have an answer to that, so she didn't say anything.

Thad exhaled, a long, windy gust of frustration, and reached for their clothing. In silence, they dressed. It took her a bit longer than it took Thad, and she was still slipping her sneakers back on when she realized he was standing in front of her. He didn't look angry anymore, but there was a puzzling intensity in the blue gaze he directed at her.

He took her hands in his and stood there, running his thumbs back and forth over her knuckles. He didn't speak, just continued to hold her hands loosely in his, searching her eyes for something. Finally she couldn't take the silence. In a near whisper, she said, "What?"

Thad's fingers stopped their restless dance across the backs of her hands. "You're important to me. Whether or not we make love every day, I still want to be married to you. Yesterday I thought...I thought you were leaving for good when you drove away."

Her pupils dilated, and he knew he'd struck close to the truth. She hesitated, as if to choose the right words. "I never left with the intention of abandoning our marriage. I thought about it. I even started to pack. But then I remembered my wedding vows. 'For better or for worse.' I said those words and I meant them." She looked away from him then, fixing her gaze on some inner vision.

"I meant them, too." He waited, but she didn't respond. "Is that it?"

"Is what it?"

"Is that the only reason you came back?" He was pushing her, but he had to know. He hoped he was right—God, he *had* to be right—but he needed to hear her say the words before he could believe them.

She still hadn't looked at him again. Her hands trembled in his and with a sudden, swift movement, she withdrew them from his clasp and crossed her arms over her breasts, tucking her hands close to her body as if she were cold. It struck him that it was an extraordinarily defensive gesture.

"Please tell me."

She heaved a deep sigh. "All right, Thad. You want to know what I'm thinking? I'm thinking that I was terribly unwise to marry you so quickly. We needed time to get to know each other, time to explore our relationship and decide—"

"I made my decision the day I looked through that window and caught you staring. You blushed, and I was hooked."

She hadn't been expecting *that*, he could tell. Her mouth hung slightly open, and she had a distinctly dazed look on her face. "The first day we met?"

He smiled wryly. "Well, it was technically our second meeting. Which brings me to another question. If you remembered me as the cad who manhandled you at that party, why are you married to that cad now?"

"First impressions can be wrong," she said primly.

"And you think you've gotten out of answering the original question. Did you only come back because it was your duty as a wife?"

She wouldn't look him in the eye. "No. Not only because of duty."

He took a deep breath and let it slowly out. "One day we're going to need something more than sex to hold us together."

Finally she looked at him. And in her eyes he saw the depths of a despair greater than anything he had imagined. The sadness that overlay it slumped her shoulders; tears welled in her eyes. "I know."

Gently he put his hands on her shoulders, massaging the tension away. "Why are you crying?" If he were the kind of man who prayed, he'd pray he knew the answer.

She shrugged; her shoulders felt fragile and delicate beneath his hands. "Reality and expectations collide in everyone's life, I suppose."

"And our marriage hasn't lived up to your expectations." He knew he deserved every lash of the mental whip with which he was flaying himself.

"It's just..." Her eyes filled with tears and she squeezed them tightly shut for a minute. "You are *not* going to do this," she said, and he realized the comment wasn't directed at him, but at herself.

He couldn't take her tears. Encircling her waist, he moved to pull her against him in comfort.

"Don't!" She tore herself away and stood beyond reach.

He was so shocked it took him a moment to recover. "Why not?"

"Because...because I don't want charity. I've accepted the limits of our relationship." Her eyes overflowed as she turned and stood with her back to him.

"*Charity?* How can putting my arms around the woman I love be charity?" He spread his hands in bewilderment and exasperation. This was going all wrong. He'd wanted to—

She had whirled around again. Her eyes were huge and serious in her face. "Did you mean that?"

It took him a moment to realize what she was talking about. "That I love you? Hell, yes, I meant that!" He took her by the shoulders, caressing her upper arms. "Why else would you be wearing my ring?"

Her eyes were shining and incredulous. "But you never said—"

"I didn't even say it to *myself* until recently." He

folded her close, and this time she came willingly, fitting against him the way only she could. "But I'm telling you now. I love you, Chloe. And starting right this minute I'm going to tell you how much you mean to me every single day for the rest of our lives." There. It hadn't been as painful as he'd expected.

Her shoulders were shaking, and he looked down at her, alarmed. "Stop crying. You're supposed to be deliriously happy now." He couldn't prevent the note of anxiety that crept into his voice. He'd just bared his soul to her; now he realized she hadn't said a word about love yet. Had he been mistaken?

Then she raised her face to his, and he saw she wasn't crying. Well, yes, she was. But through her tears her smile was brilliant. "You asked me a question that I still haven't answered."

For a moment, he went blank. Then he remembered. "I think—I *hope*—I know the answer, but you tell me, anyway. Why did you decide not to leave me yesterday?"

As he rocked her back and forth, she played with the curling hairs that escaped the neck of his T-shirt. "I decided to stay because I love you. Because I wanted to spend the rest of my life with you even if you couldn't love me the same way." She pressed a kiss into the hollow of his throat, making him shiver.

He tightened his arms around her and swung her in a wide circle, holding his world in his arms. He might not have much experience with "forever," but he recognized it now. She humbled him and delighted him, and he thanked God she'd looked past the man she'd met initially, the man who'd been trouble with a capital *T*. His name might still start with that letter, but his lady loved him. It made all the difference in the world.

Epilogue

"What if it's a girl?" Thad rubbed his hand gently over the swollen mound of his wife's belly. "Should we call her Luke-retia?"

"Very funny." Chloe shook her head definitely. "This is Luke. A mother knows these things. But if the next one is a girl, she's going to be Ruth Anne. Ruth is the Biblical woman in the story that kept me from walking out on you."

"Thank God you didn't." It was a fervent prayer. He leaned forward and gently touched his lips to hers.

A crash from the kitchen had both of them whipping their heads around in alarm. "You'd better get in there and see what's keeping Matthew and Mark so fascinated. The last time they were quiet for this long was the day they flushed my pearl earrings down the potty."

Thad laughed as he got to his feet. "I notice you

haven't left your jewelry lying around in the bathroom anymore.''

As he walked into the kitchen to see what his sons were up to, her heart flipped in her chest just like it had that day, the day she'd seen him standing in her window at the old church. After almost two-and-a-half years of marriage, she felt luckier than any woman had a right to be.

They'd waited just long enough to ensure that anyone who could count would know she and Thad hadn't "had" to get married. The twins would be seventeen months old next week, two precocious terrors with their father's blond curls. They moved through life like miniature tornadoes, leaving everyone in their path gaping in disbelief and thanking God the damage wasn't worse.

They'd been only ten months old when she'd realized that she was going to be a mother again. So much for the rumor that breastfeeding women didn't get pregnant. Thad had been delighted. She was, too, after she got over the shock.

Her father was the epitome of the doting grandpa, and he'd taken the news of the new baby better than she had. Thad's mother had passed away two weeks after Chloe learned of her second pregnancy, but their grief had been tempered by her happiness at having the chance to see her first two grandsons. Margreta had refused to let them mope in her presence. She had never expected to live long enough to see one grandchild, much less two, she said, and it was cause for joy rather than sorrow.

Four of her former lovers came to her funeral and wound up consoling each other, much to Chloe's amazement. Her own father had performed a beautiful and touching service that celebrated Margreta's life; and the twins, whom they hadn't been able to bring themselves to leave in the hands of a baby-sitter, had slept through the entire thing. Which had amazed them all.

And in about two weeks, another little Shippen would enter the world. Life came full circle, she thought.

Another louder crash made her jump in the recliner where she sat. Thad's voice sounded harried, and although she couldn't make out the exact words, the tone told her that Daddy needed reinforcements.

Letting down the footrest, she scooted herself forward to the edge of the chair just as Thad appeared in the doorway, a squirming toddler in each arm. All three of them wore liberal coats of what appeared to be flour, and she struggled to keep a straight face as she slowly rose to her feet and waddled toward them.

An unexpected popping sensation warned her, mere instants before a gush of fluid spilled down her legs and created a spreading puddle on the polished wood floor of the family room. Her slippers were soaking wet and the puddle inched precariously close to the Oriental rug they'd purchased only a month ago.

"Your water broke!" Thad leaped forward, then lurched to a halt. "But it's two weeks too early."

"You want to explain that to Luke?"

He wheeled and ran back into the kitchen, returning with a roll of paper towels, which he tossed at her. "Here. Let me call your father to manage these monkeys, and I'll take you to the hospital."

"Mommy tinkled!" Matthew crowed.

"Tinkled onna f'oor," pronounced his brother.

Paper towels. She was giggling helplessly as she caught the roll just before it hit her in the face. Only a man would use paper towels at a time like this. She hoped he had about a hundred more rolls ready.

Thad had promised her the rest of their lives together, but he hadn't warned her about the wild ride along the way. She should have known, she thought, as love swelled within her. With a man like Thad, nothing would ever be predictable.

She smiled to herself, then sucked in a breath as a contraction tightened her belly with surprising intensity. It would be in keeping with the unorthodox Shippen family character if this baby were born on the floor, or in the car on the way to the hospital.

Oh, well. She'd resigned herself to raised eyebrows long ago. It was a small price to pay for love that would last a lifetime.

* * * * * *

Take 2 bestselling love stories FREE

Plus get a FREE surprise gift!

Special Limited-Time Offer

Mail to Silhouette Reader Service™

3010 Walden Avenue
P.O. Box 1867
Buffalo, N.Y. 14240-1867

YES! Please send me 2 free Silhouette Desire® novels and my free surprise gift. Then send me 6 brand-new novels every month, which I will receive months before they appear in bookstores. Bill me at the low price of $3.12 each plus 25¢ delivery and applicable sales tax, if any.* That's the complete price, and a saving of over 10% off the cover prices—quite a bargain! I understand that accepting the books and gift places me under no obligation ever to buy any books. I can always return a shipment and cancel at any time. Even if I never buy another book from Silhouette, the 2 free books and the surprise gift are mine to keep forever.

225 SEN CH7U

Name	(PLEASE PRINT)
Address	Apt. No.
City	State	Zip

the beloved miniseries by
USA Today **bestselling author**

Cait London

continues with
RAFE PALLADIN:
MAN OF SECRETS

(SD #1160)

Available August 1998

When takeover tycoon Rafe Palladin set out to *acquire* Demi Tallchief as part of a business deal, Demi had a few conditions of her own. And Rafe had some startling secrets to reveal....

"Cait London is one of the best writers in contemporary romance today."   —*Affaire de Coeur*

And coming from Desire in **December 1998,** look for **The Perfect Fit** in which *Man of the Month* Nick Palladin lures Ivory Tallchief back home to Amen Flats, Wyoming.

Available at your favorite retail outlet.

MEN at WORK

All work and no play?
Not these men!

July 1998
MACKENZIE'S LADY by Dallas Schulze

Undercover agent Mackenzie Donahue's
lazy smile and deep blue eyes were his best
weapons. But after rescuing—and kissing!—
damsel in distress Holly Reynolds, how could
he betray her by spying on her brother?

August 1998
MISS LIZ'S PASSION by Sherryl Woods

Todd Lewis could put up a building with ease,
but quailed at the sight of a classroom! Still,
Liz Gentry, his son's teacher, was no battle-ax,
and soon Todd started planning some
extracurricular activities of his own....

September 1998
A CLASSIC ENCOUNTER
by Emilie Richards

Doctor Chris Matthews was intelligent, sexy
and *very* good with his hands—which made
him all the more dangerous to single mom
Lizette St. Hilaire. So how long could she
resist Chris's special brand of TLC?

Available at your favorite retail outlet!

MEN AT WORK™

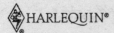 HARLEQUIN®  *Silhouette*®

Look us up on-line at: http://www.romance.net   PMAW2

HERE COME THE

Virgin Brides!

Celebrate the joys of first love with more unforgettable stories from Romance's brightest stars:

SWEET BRIDE OF REVENGE
by Suzanne Carey—June 1998 (SR #1300)

Reader favorite Suzanne Carey weaves a sensuously powerful tale about a man who forces the daughter of his enemy to be his bride of revenge. But what happens when this hard-hearted husband falls head over heels…for his wife?

THE BOUNTY HUNTER'S BRIDE
by Sandra Steffen—July 1998 (SR #1306)

In this provocative page-turner by beloved author Sandra Steffen, a shotgun wedding is only the beginning when an injured bounty hunter and the sweet seductress who'd nursed him to health are discovered in a remote mountain cabin by her gun-toting dad and *four* brothers!

SUDDENLY…MARRIAGE!
by Marie Ferrarella—August 1998 (SR #1312)

RITA Award-winning author Marie Ferrarella weaves a magical story set in sultry New Orleans about two people determined to remain single who exchange vows in a mock ceremony during Mardi Gras, only to learn their bogus marriage is the real thing….

And look for more VIRGIN BRIDES in future months, only in—

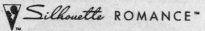

Available at your favorite retail outlet.

 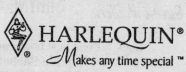